Strangehold

Crossroads of Worlds
Book One

Rene Sears

Brown Dog Press

Book Layout © 2017 BookDesignTemplates.com
Cover Design © 2017 Lou Harper http://louharper.com/Design.html

Strangehold/ Rene Sears. -- 978-1546618195

To Ben,
always my first reader

CONTENTS

MATTHEW

Water slapped against the side of the boat. Matthew pulled the oars hard, pulse beating in his throat.

The boat rocked into shore, bottom catching on sand. Matthew pulled in breath and waited. He needed to set foot on the shore, but he couldn't make himself. He hovered, hands clenched on the boat's edge, then pushed himself out.

His foot splashed into shallow water. No one died. He stepped onto land.

No matter what happened next, it was a sweet step.

His toes curled in wet sand. He pulled a loaded backpack from the boat, stepped forward again. And again.

Isabel had begged him not to go, but in this, as so many other things, he'd had to disappoint her. Maybe, once he was dead, she could find some reconciliation with her family. But, against the odds, he was not dead yet.

It had been a gamble, coming here. Even now, the Council's curse tightened about his neck like a collar. It would become a noose if he set foot on the mainland, but this island didn't—quite—count. Or so he had hoped, and it seemed he had been right. Now he had one last chance to finish the job he'd started nearly twenty years before.

He wondered, briefly, if his old teacher or his fellows would be able to tell it had been him, but he dismissed the thought. The spell had been years in the planning—it was his life's work—but at this point, result was more important than recognition.

He used a brief wisp of magic to send the boat back out into deeper water where it could drift until someone found it. The hot white sand was pleasant beneath his feet. On his island, there were only pebbles on the shores. Music and occasional shrieks of laughter drifted from further down the beach. A lighthouse rose above the trees, striped in black and white. He pulled a twist of light around himself so that no one could see him. Even Isabel's eyes would've slipped by.

The steps up the lighthouse were cool and shaded against his bare feet. He put one foot after another; as he did, he found he missed the light.

He reached the top, and cast a spell of aversion. All the tourists fled, fleeing down the steps as if they'd found the top landing full of vomit, and he was alone with his hatred.

Sometimes, in his weaker moments, he feared it was only a grudge. Once he'd had a sister—once he'd had one person in all the world who loved him. Sometimes he felt no other love since then had mattered.

His parents had been profligate in their trade with Faerie, carrying bespelled items across the gates, selling to the fae, and then back to the spellcasters who traded in their goods. Perhaps they thought of their fae contacts as friends, or thought their usefulness would keep them safe.

It didn't.

Changelings were not supposed to happen anymore—long ago, a healthy babe might be replaced by a sickly fae simulacrum and the babe raised in Faerie, but now there were treaties between overhill and under meant to prevent it.

Once he knew a trader, a tall man with pale braids, who had juggled balls of light to make him and his sister laugh, who had given them sweets and told them stories of the creatures that lived in the deep forests of Faerie. He had liked the man, until one day his sister disappeared from their campsite. Only after the fae become involved and took the search to Faerie did they find the man with the braids, and with him, Matthew's sister.

The fae had punished the man. He had been forbidden his trade, and whipped by the Queen's Blade until his back was flayed, and cursed to bear the wound unhealing for five decades, to show the human Council that the Faerie queen took breaking the treaty seriously.

Long ago, they stole babies, and maybe an infant took Faerie in stride. His sister had been ten, and she was never the same afterwards. She startled at things that weren't there, and flinched away from him and his family. She had nightmares. When she was fifteen, she killed herself. They found her drowned face-down in a duck pond she could easily have crawled out of, if only she had wanted to. His parents eventually divorced; his life had been turned upside down; the sister he loved was dead.

The fae who'd stolen her had been punished. In the eyes of the fae court and the Council, justice had been done. In his eyes, not remotely.

But this wasn't about revenge; at least, not solely.

Spellcasters and fae weren't meant to be as close as they'd become. They were literally from different worlds, and though they had reached an uneasy truce, for centuries they had been predator and prey.

The problem, as he saw it, was that people liked to lie to themselves. They wanted to believe the fae were friendly, that only monsters stole children, that the queen really had put away her Blade.

The only way to save them from themselves was to break the truce irreparably and expose the fae as the monsters they were. One could remember a laughing tall man with pale braids giving candy to traders' children. One must also remember that the same man stole sisters and returned them shattered beyond repair.

His hands clenched into fists. He exhaled, slowly, and made them relax. It was not only his sister—it was everyone's sister, everyone's child.

He opened his backpack and pulled out what he needed: the diagram he'd worked out what felt like ages ago, chalk for the circle, a silver charm in the shape of a frog that Isabel had given him years before, when things had been good between them. The leyline here was powerful, much stronger than the thin power on his island, and he allowed himself a moment to revel in it before he got to work.

He chalked the initial lines of the circle and hesitated for only a moment before he crushed the frog charm in his fist, aided by the application of a little magical force. Magic poured out of it. He kept drawing.

No one would thank him for what he did here—if anyone ever knew what he had done. But maybe future generations, free from the fear of fae allies turning on them, could breathe a little easier. *Isabel, I'm sorry for all of it.* He chalked the final lines, checked them against his diagram, drew on the power of the ley, and cast his spell.

MORGAN

The last time I saw my sister, Gwen was hugely, radiantly pregnant, and asking me to be happy for her. This time she was hunched over a coffee, wan and tired, while the twins stacked blocks and knocked them over at her feet. As I tried to find the right words, one girl knocked over the other's tower before she was done building, and a squall of anger disrupted their play, a brief tempest of disappointment that the world wasn't going according to her plan.

I knew exactly how she felt.

Shadows ringed Gwen's eyes, proof of sleepless nights, but a darker circle marred her left eye, bruise-purple even beneath the heavy foundation she had smeared over it in a futile attempt at concealment. No amount of makeup could hide the swelling; her left eye looked half asleep, while her right was haunted, searching. She winced as she took a sip of coffee and I stopped searching for the right words and let the wrong ones come out, the ones I'd been trying not to say.

"I'll kill him."

Gwen stared at me, then burst out laughing, and some of the tension left the knot between my shoulder blades. If Gwen could still laugh like that, maybe things would be all right, somehow. "Ow." Gwen winced again, touching the puffy flesh at her eye socket. "Oh, Morgan, it's not Elm. He would never do this to me. It's *her*."

I leaned back and tugged at my sleeves, hoping to smooth down the gooseflesh before my sister noticed. There was only one person Gwen would refer to solely by a pronoun like that.

Gloriana, the queen of the fae.

I had only had the dubious pleasure of seeing the queen once before, and it was not an experience I was eager to repeat. I had never really understood how Gwen could bear to live in Faerie. "She can't. You're the ambassador from the Association."

Gwen's lips twisted, as though she'd tasted something far bitterer than coffee. "That doesn't mean as much as it did."

One of the girls squealed at my feet, and I leaned down to pass back the block that had gotten caught in the cuff of my trouser leg. Dread curled in my stomach, churning the heat of my drink into ice. "What happened?"

"I don't know exactly. She thinks someone overhill is trying to attack Faerie. She thinks I know something. She sent one of her enforcers to ask me about it."

I winced and stirred my coffee. The fragile peace between human and fae had lasted four decades. I had no desire to see it slip away. My mentor, Marcus, had told me stories of how it had been before the truce: will o' the wisps and phoukas luring the innocent to their deaths, duels between fae knights and human spellcasters, fae raids against human towns, using glamour to lure people into Faerie. The Queen's Blade carting off casters in the night, or leaving them dead where they slept.

Not that humans had never been aggressors, but before metal became widespread, we'd had little defense. The tide had turned around the industrial revolution, and stories of the fae became myth and superstition. The general human population had been able to forget that Faerie had ever been a threat, that Faerie ever existed.

Those of us with magic never had.

"Does she think *you* had anything to do with it? Or the Association? There will always be idiots, but she has to know no one official would do anything to endanger the truce."

Gwen's smile was old, or maybe that was the swollen eye. "Does it matter? She sees a threat."

"How can I help you?"

Gwen's shoulders relaxed infinitesimally. The hesitation stung, though it shouldn't. I had made no secret of my disapproval of her choices. Gwen's fingers tightened around her coffee cup. She looked at the web of cracks in the plaster of my kitchen ceiling as if she could find answers there. "I'm not worried about myself." Gwen went on before I could say anything. "Oh, there's plenty that could go wrong for me, I know that. It's just that it's too late to fade back into the shadows. She knows me. If she's angry with me, there's nothing any of us can do about it—not you, not me, and not Elm. It's them I worry about." She turned her head until she was facing the twins crawling around on the ground. "Look at them, Morgan. You've barely glanced at them since we got here."

"Your black eye distracted me." She shook her head. I

steeled myself and looked under the table.

They were beautiful children, but then, they would be. I had long since decided that children weren't in the cards for me, but I'd looked forward to nieces or nephews to spoil. That had been before Gwen lost her head over a lord of the high court of Faerie. I hoped that remained just a metaphor.

Time was funny underhill; to me, it had only been six months since I'd seen Gwen pregnant, but the girls were toddlers already. I regretted not knowing what they had looked like when they were babies. They were still chubby, still clumsy with their youth, but even without caster's sight, I could see the people they would become in their faces. Those people weren't human—not entirely.

Instead, their high cheekbones and slightly pointed ears showed the fae heritage from their father. Their mother was present too: the sweep of hair, the rounded jaw—human traits. They'd have to be older to see if they'd be able to pass for human in the mundane world. They'd never be able to in the fae court, whose residents could read their magic as easily as look at them, but it was different there; they had always welcomed changelings, while overhill had tried its best to forget Faerie when Faerie withdrew in response to the rising tide of iron in the world above.

But she hadn't meant *just* look at them. I summoned spellsight and saw the girls and everything else in my kitchen overlaid with faint traces of silver. A leyline would have been bright silver, but no line of power in my house was that strong. Magic was like water. It flowed downhill, and it followed the path of least resistance, but unlike bodies of water, it existed at least slightly almost every place on earth. Leylines were like rivers, but the magic free-flowing in my house was more like a sprinkling of droplets: there wasn't enough of it to be useful. That was all right; every caster had her own way of compensating for the thin places. Mine were mostly inked on my skin.

The girls were still busy playing, so I could watch them unobserved. The traces of silver were maybe a little denser than they would have been in a human, unmagical child, but most of us didn't come into our abilities until later in life, so that didn't mean anything.

My sister watched me watch them. I glanced at her. "So who's who?"

"Igraine is darker, and Iliesa is fair."

I shot her a smile; our entire lives people had refused to believe we were sisters. Gwen was like our mother, pale and fair, while I took more after our father, a tall, dark, and British Arthurian scholar at Johns Hopkins.

"If anything happens to me, I want them to go to you."

She didn't look at me, and I was glad. I wasn't sure what my face looked like. Was this a presentiment of doom? "What about Elm?"

Gwen rubbed the bridge of her nose. "I don't know that he'd be able to protect them the way you would. He's of the court, and he wouldn't be comfortable taking them overhill, and if they were anywhere underhill, she'd be able to find them."

"What are you worried she'll do to them?"

"I don't know." Gwen hesitated. "A week ago, I'd have said nothing, and thought no one in Faerie would harm them. But that was before..." She touched her black eye and shrugged.

"All right, then. Just—don't let anything happen to you. I'd be a terrible mother."

"I'm not asking you to be their mother." Gwen tried to smile, but with the bruise along the ridge of her cheekbone it looked like a scowl. "I want you to be their aunt, if they need it."

"I promise."

"I want to make it official." I frowned, not exactly understanding. She misunderstood and thought I was offended. "Not for you! Not for you. I trust you." She blinked rapidly, the brittle edge of her composure fracturing. "If it—if something goes wrong and Elm can't help them, I want them tied to you and not the court."

"Of course." I swallowed the lump in my throat.

Gwen leaned down to the girls. "Iliesa. Igraine. I need you to pay attention to your auntie Morgan." They turned eyes on her, one set Gwen's dark brown, the other a brilliant grass green, and then looked as one to me. They seemed unnaturally focused for children that small, but then I didn't know many toddlers.

"Girls, let me hold your hands." Iliesa immediately put her warm hand in mine, while Igraine measured me with her eyes for a moment, then took my other hand. How strange did I look to them, used as they were to more angular fae faces, and glamour all around them? Magic was different in Faerie; underhill was so much smaller than earth, magic filled it and permeated it. There were no thin places, and conversely no leyline rivers of power. Did overhill look different to them, empty of the magic they breathed like air at home?

I was stalling. I took a breath and cleared my mind of everything except what I needed to do. Gwen said she wanted me to be their aunt if they needed me, but I was already that. They needed a guardian, in the old sense. I pulled a thread of energy from the tattoo over my heart, a stylized oak tree—for something this important, personal energy felt right, and this energy, kept against my skin, was the most personal I had—and sent a tendril unfurling toward the girls. When I was young, I'd have used a drop of blood, but I was older and subtler now.

"I promise fidelity. I promise protection. If you need me, I promise I will be there." There were more complicated oaths I could have sworn, but this felt right. I sent a surge of silver power from the tattoo over my heart to the two of them, binding myself to the words I spoke. Both sets of eyes, dark brown and improbable green, widened. They had both felt it. They glanced down in unison at their left hands. *It's not creepy. They're my nieces.*

So they had felt that, too. "Look, Gwen. Igraine, turn your hand up so your mother can see your palm."

Gwen and frowned and bent over Igraine's hand, the ends of her red-blond hair brushing over her daughter. "I don't see anything."

"Good." I rummaged through a drawer past unopened kitchen scissors and balls of twine until I found a magnifying glass. "Now look through this."

Gwen's right eye widened as she took it in. "I thought it was a freckle, but it's...an acorn?" She glanced at me.

Gwen had seen my oak tattoo. "Both of them?"

"You asked for my protection. They have it. I hope they never need it."

Gwen pulled me into a hug, her vertebrae all too fragile beneath my fingertips. "Thank you. I hope so too. But it gives me peace, just in case."

"Just in case," I echoed.

The girls seemed to take the magic in stride. They went back to their blocks, two heads bent together, black hair next to pale gold, the color of our mother's. Gwen and I sat back at the table, and I poured another cup of coffee.

"You should come visit," Gwen said, hands wrapped around her coffee cup. She very carefully looked at her knuckles.

"I'd love to," I said, not entirely truthfully, "but I can't. The queen—"

"The queen has not forbidden visitors from overhill. You could come. Just for a day or so, to see the girls."

I took a sip of coffee to cover my hesitation.

I did want to know the girls better, and for them to know me. I had never been to Faerie—Gwen had always come to see me overhill.

I could feel the girls now, and I always would be able to, until and unless they ever wanted me to dissolve the bond. This close, I was aware of their location, but when they went back to Faerie, all I'd be able to tell was whether they were okay.

My reasons for not wanting to go to Faerie hadn't changed. But the reasons I should do it anyway had become more important.

"I will," I said slowly. "And I'll keep coming back. Someone's going to have to teach them how to use the human side of their magic."

The smile that broke over her face was like sunrise. "I always hoped you'd come see me there." Only then did I realize I'd been thinking about Faerie all wrong. Being there was not something she forced herself to bear. It was her home now; whether or not I wanted to think of it that way, she obviously did. She didn't ask why I'd never come to see it—she never had. Maybe she didn't want to know the answer. But I couldn't bear her thinking it was anything to do with her.

"Do you remember the trial?" I didn't have to say which one.

She frowned. "Of course. But what does that have to do with anything?"

It had been eighteen years before, the one time I saw the queen of Faerie in person. She had worn a gold dress, her midnight hair bound up with strands of gold. Her face had been cool and merciless as she stared at the human man who had attacked her nephew. I had been in the audience, but as her gaze swept the room, I felt irrationally sure that she'd marked me out.

Behind her stood the Queen's Blade, in golden armor that matched her dress. The Blade hadn't been wielded against humans since the truce went into effect, but that didn't make him any less intimidating. His helm was carved with leaves and vines and two great sweeping horns—or possibly, as he was fae, the horns weren't part of the helm. It covered his head so that all I could see of his face was the uncompromising line of his mouth. I was almost certain throughout the trial that the queen would demand her Blade dole out the punishment, but she didn't.

When the trial finished, I stood with my mentor, Marcus, as fae dignitaries streamed past us. I kept my head down, but I watched surreptitiously out of the corner of my eyes. Lords and ladies, nearly human-looking, slightly inhuman, and entirely other paraded by. They spread rainbow wings, they walked on hooves, they tossed hair in shades not found in nature that I'd have to shell out a fortune at a salon to achieve. At last, only the Council of the Association and their apprentices stood by, one less apprentice next to me than once there had been.

The queen and her silent escort stalked past the other members of the Council without glancing at them. But at Marcus, she stopped. I kept my head down, barely breathing.

"He was your student," she said to Marcus. Her voice rang like bells, cold as winter, cold as death.

"He was, your majesty," he said, bowing his head. His voice was rough with grief. I wondered if she could hear it. If she did, let her think it was for the transgression, and not for the condemned. "I am sorry for it."

She stayed still a moment longer. I glanced up, unable to help myself. The queen's eyes were fixed on Marcus, her mouth twisted in a sneer, but the golden helm had turned toward me. I dropped my gaze to my feet hastily.

"You are not welcome," she said to Marcus, "in the lands beneath the hills. You are not welcome in the Shining Courts."

"Your majesty," he said, bowing his head even further. From her angle to the front of him, she wouldn't be able to see the muscle jumping at the side of his jaw as he clenched it. "I would not presume."

She swept on. I looked at her back and saw her Blade still looking at me—or at Marcus—eyes hard through the slit in his helm. In the eighteen years since, I had never forgotten the look in them. I'd never forgotten the threat. It hadn't seemed worth the risk.

"At the trial," I told my sister, "the queen was adamant that Marcus never darken her doorstep. I was right there; I've always assumed she meant me too."

Gwen laughed, then winced, a hand going to her eye. "Morgan. Look. No offense, but the queen has no idea who you are. She knew who Marcus was, sure, but I don't think she'd see mere students as important enough to care about."

"It was a mere student on trial," I said softly. "You weren't there; you didn't see her. Or her Blade."

Gwen leaned back and wrapped her hands around her coffee cup. "Well, she no longer has a Blade. He left her service not long after the trial, so you don't have to worry about that—anyway, the treaty forbids it."

"If you say it won't be a problem, I believe you. You'd know far better than me." A coil of unease crept up my spine nonetheless. But truly, the queen *had* been talking to Marcus, not me. One of the girls—Igraine—crawled over my foot to retrieve a block, and I told myself to suck it up—they needed me to come, so I was going to.

"I'll get Elm's family to ask the queen. I'm not in her good graces at the moment, but she wouldn't refuse a request from them."

I nodded, hiding a frown with a sip of coffee. There was another reason I didn't want to go to Faerie, but there was no need to tell Gwen about it. She and Elm had had two weddings—one in Faerie, and one overhill. It was at the latter where I'd first met her smiling, golden husband and his smiling, golden family. Over champagne and cake a forbidding older woman had cornered me and asked question after question about Gwen's childhood, her education, her ambitions, until finally, half amused, half annoyed, I'd told her to ask Gwen herself if she wanted to know.

The woman looked down her long nose at me and dropped her glamour, there in the reception hall. In front of me was a formidable fae woman of indeterminate age, golden hair tipped with purple twisted in a complicated updo held in place with jeweled pins. "I am asking *you*," she said, "for insight into your sister—such as you have to offer. If my nephew insists on marrying so far beneath himself I will do what I must to make the best of it."

I counted to ten, and then did it again. It didn't help. "Somehow I doubt your nephew would agree with your assessment, and if he does, better they not marry at all."

She shot me a sideways glance as her glamour turned her into something more human but no less cranky. "I know who you are, Morgan Tenpenny, sister of Guinevere, student of Marcus Grey. You do your sister no favors with your connection."

I had never told Gwen about it, and I wasn't going to now. If she didn't already know how little Elm's family thought of her, why should I tell her? And if they were so stupid as to think of her badly, what should I care for them? But it was different, now that the girls were in the picture. I had stayed away because of fear of the queen's retribution, because I was Marcus's student; and because as Marcus's student, I could only lower my sister in their estimation. Out of sight, out of mind, or so I had hoped. To be completely honest, I hadn't been entirely comfortable with my sister's marriage. I'm sure Elm loved her and she him, but their marriage had put her literally out of my world.

No, I realized now. That was wrong. Her choice to be an ambassador to Faerie had done that before she ever met him. She had been willing to keep one foot in both worlds to stay in touch with me. The only question was how willing I was to reach back to her.

"When should I come?" I said.

"Give me a few weeks. Say, the next new moon. That'll give me time to make the arrangements." My sister smiled at me, and her face glowed despite the bruise around her eye.

If she said she could get her family to make it right with the queen, then I believed her. "I'll look forward to it," I told her.

A small hand tugged the edge of my shirt. Iliesa had brought a stack of blocks to show us, babbling in a toddler approximation of speech, brown eyes intent on me. I swung her up into my lap and ran a hand over her soft golden hair. The tiny acorn on her hand was a reminder of my promise to her and her sister.

"We have to get back," Gwen said softly.

"Of course," I said. "But I'll see you soon."

I drove them back to the feygate in Cheaha State Park. It wasn't too far—I had moved here with the feygate in mind. We went down a road not marked on any map and hiked down the trail to the gate. They stood in the middle of the rough stone arch, silver energy floating like fog around the gate and the trees around it even in sunshine. Gwen held the girls' hands, a picture of maternal affection framed by the gate. She looked over her shoulder at me as they crossed. I would pass through myself before too long. I told myself the uneasy shudder that ran along my skin was only the magic of the feygate.

When I got home, I cracked a beer, though it wasn't even three in the afternoon yet, and held the cold glass, slick with condensation, against my forehead. A long gulp of brown ale slid down my throat. I set the bottle down, opened the pantry, and pulled out a cardboard cylinder that had once held breadcrumbs. The plastic top popped off with no effort at all, and I pulled out my sidheblade, cold as ice and glowing with restrained fire to my spellcaster's sight. It looked like a silver bracelet now, but it would come to my hand as dagger or axe—whatever I needed. I had not had to use it as a sword in years. I hoped I'd never have to again, but...

I flipped through my calendar and marked the next new moon: three weeks, about. It had been years since I used a gate—and I'd only used the ones that went from here to there overhill, not the ones that crossed into Faerie—but I'd do it for Gwen. I couldn't wait another six months to see the girls, not with how fast they were growing. I supposed I'd have to see Elm's family again, but that couldn't be helped. For Gwen's sake, I'd try to get along with them. At least Elm himself had been courteous the few times we'd met.

And if we were all very lucky, the queen would have other things on her mind. She had promised her Blade would never again attack humans when the peace between our worlds went into effect forty years before, but as Gwen's bruised face attested, she had other ways of expressing her displeasure.

I hoped my sister and her family would bear no more of it.

*

Weeks went past and I could feel the girls, a faint, tenuous connection when they were Underhill, but strong enough to know they didn't need me as guardian. I'd be happy if they never did; they would need me in other ways. They were fae, but they were human, too, and a spellcaster's gifts were their birthright. They were young yet, but the better they knew me, the easier their teaching would be when they were older. Trust all around could only help.

The day before I was to go, the waning crescent moon rose in the afternoon sky, a sliver of white against clear blue. The sun's rays dyed it blood red, a trick of the light that left me uneasy all evening. I'd kept my tattoos filled with magic so I'd never need to be close to a leyline to work, but I checked them again anyway; they were brimming with energy, just as they'd been the last time I checked. I made sure of my wards and packed for Underhill: clothes, food from the mortal realm, charms and runestones, three sticks of incense. The sidheblade rested against my wrist, to all appearances an innocent silver bangle.

I was as ready as I could be.

I slept fitfully until midnight, tossed out of amorphous bad dreams that slithered away as I woke. A sound that wasn't a sound echoed in my skull like a bell that had been struck much too hard. All the lines of my wards vibrated, and the tattoo above my heart reverberated worst of all. Igraine. Iliesa.

The oath that I'd sworn bound me to them, and I sent my magic sense questing down it. The line between us was taut, but they were safe. Safe-ish. I closed my eyes and traced the lines of magic from my little wards down the thicker leylines to the powerful river of energy that led to the feygate in Cheaha. There, the magic terminated abruptly.

I couldn't go to Gwen and the girls.

The feygate had slammed shut.

All right; that was just the closest one. There were others—a longer drive away, but I could get there, and sooner if I left now.

I pulled on my jeans and shoved my feet into my boots. At least I was already packed. I settled my bracelet and scooped up my tool bag, a backpack stuffed with the this-and-that human casters needed to work more complicated spells.

The phone rang.

My heartbeat sped and I dropped the bag on my foot. I swore as I fumbled the phone from my pocket and swept my thumb across the screen. "Hello?"

"Morgan?" Eliza Bent spoke in my ear. She was head of the Spellcasters' Association of New York, SCANY for short but more often known as the Association; in earlier years the Gentlemen Protectorate, until sometime in the thirties or so when they got to the point where a considerable number of the members were female. I was not a member, but I helped them out when I could. Eliza and I went way back. We'd been the last pupils of Marcus Grey before he stopped teaching, along with his most infamous student, Matthew March. She and I shared the bond of people who'd been through the same crucible. "What the fuck is going on?"

"I don't know."

"Have you heard anything from your sister?"

I closed my eyes. "About a month ago, but I told you about that."

"Yes, and she told me as well. I meant tonight."

"No." I tried to swallow. "I was going to see her tomorrow." My gaze dropped to my useless suitcase.

"Morgan." Eliza's voice went gentle. "All the feygates are shut."

"All of them? I know the one closest to me is, but I hoped..."

"All of them. The one upstate is also guarded."

"Guarded?"

"A phouka is circling it, braying at the night sky. The nearest caster's not answering his phone."

No one could have slept through what I'd felt. And a phouka wasn't easy to ignore either. Eliza needed to get someone over there before the police got involved with something they were totally unequipped to handle. Under terms of the treaty between underhill and over, nonmagical humans ought to be sacrosanct, but, well. The gates were supposed to stay open too. "What do you need me to do?"

"I *want* you to come here and help me." For one brief moment, I heard the girl I'd studied with twenty years ago. Then Eliza's voice firmed. "But I *need* you to check out the feygates nearest you. Some of them might be guarded as well. Maybe one of the guards can tell us what the hell is going on."

I nodded, though of course she couldn't see me. "They're far apart. I'm going to call in some help." Feygates were set up along leylines, because of the energy needed to maintain them. Casters usually lived pretty close to leylines, too, because they liked having ample magic to work with. I didn't like all of them, and some of them I didn't know all that well, but most of them would help me out. Whatever was going on, we needed all the help we could get.

Eliza bit back something. "People you trust."

Well, duh. "Of course."

"Call me as soon as you find out anything. Anything at all. I don't want this to be another fuck-up like the Matthew incident."

"I will. You too," I said, but Eliza had already hung up. Only she would call a crisis of interspecies diplomacy a fuck-up. A brief memory of Matthew flickered in front of me: him tracing an intricate knot-like glyph on a bar napkin, his face mobile with excitement. I shoved it away. He had made his own bed, and he wasn't my business anymore.

Anyone with even the mildest sensitivity would have felt the feygates close, but the first three practitioners I called didn't answer their phones. Unease cramped my stomach. I left brief messages with each of them while the kettle boiled, then poured hot water over coffee grounds in my French press. I was too anxious to feel tired, but there was nothing like a few hours behind the wheel in the middle of the night to unwind me, and then I'd need the caffeine.

I dialed a fourth number, and relief at getting an answer kept me from snapping back at the terse "What?"

"Anil!"

"What do you want, Morgan?"

"The feygates—Eliza says they're all closed. Is yours—?"

"Yes." Anil lived outside of San Antonio, close to the Lost Maples feygate and attendant leyline. "All of them?"

"The one by me is, and Eliza says the one in the Adirondacks has some kind of guard—a phouka."

I heard him turn from the phone and spit. I raised an eyebrow, though he couldn't see it. Anil wasn't part of the Association either—he disapproved of that many casters together—but he got on pretty well with the fae. Then again, a phouka alone was worth spitting. Anil was older than me. He might remember incidents from before the treaty. "There's nothing haunting the one by me—it's just shut."

"Let me know if anything changes, will you? Or Eliza—do you have her number?"

"I'll call you," he said firmly. "They don't care about us down here, Morgan; you should know that by now."

I could have told him that Eliza had called me, not the other way around, but it wasn't an argument I wanted to get into, and I was so relieved that someone had finally answered the phone I didn't care what he thought about the Association. "All right, Anil. I'm headed to the gate in Cheaha, so I'll let you know if there's anything there."

I yanked open the junk drawer that always stuck and cursed when it opened smoothly and hit me in the hip. I had a couple of maps of the southeast marked with red sharpie. American feygates were in state and national parks, for the most part, far from cities. I had a lot of driving to do unless some of my people called me back. I poured coffee into a travel mug, grabbed my tool bag, and left.

My pickup truck had three-quarters of a tank. Eliza had laughed when she'd seen it and I'd told her it was protective coloration, but the fact of the matter was that I could haul a body if need be, and anyway, it fit right in here. My home was comfortable but I hadn't put down much in the way of roots, if I thought about it; I knew my nearest neighbors well enough to nod at and say hello, but I'd never had anyone over to dinner. I worked two jobs, both online; one, designing websites for clients, was done mostly via email and phone calls, and the other, magical research with a collaborator in Vancouver, required at most a couple of meetings in person per year. It was a solitary existence, but most of the time, I didn't mind. If nothing else, it made it easier to spellcast.

My little piece of nowhere was right on the border of Georgia and Alabama, so the closest gate was in Cheaha State Park. The truck tires kicked up dust and pebbles until the gravel road turned into blacktop. I wound past sleeping houses and closed businesses until I hit I-20 and headed west.

The highway zipped by, reflective white stripes shimmering brighter beneath orange lights and dimming between them, for just me and truckers hauling loads. I didn't have too far to go to get to the park—I'd chosen my house with that in mind. The last forty years of official peace between fae and human hadn't been without incident, and a caster near the gate cut down response time if someone or something inimical came through.

Once I turned off the highway the roads got narrower and darker. Signs directing me to the park flashed green and white in the beams from my headlights and disappeared. I had to slow down as the road curved upward, and now the signs pointed me toward trailheads, toward camping, toward scenic views. I ignored them and turned onto a gravel service road. Here was another good reason to like my truck—though the road wasn't well-maintained, I bounced over the ruts with no problems. The park rangers would have been distressed to see the poor condition of the road, if they ever noticed it. Once or twice a year I came out and made sure the ward was still working to keep people away.

About a mile into the woods, I parked. The truck engine ticked in the cool night air. An owl called somewhere in the distance. I pulled a flashlight out of my bag and flicked it on, slung the tool bag over my shoulder, and started walking. It felt good to stretch my legs. It might be the last pleasant thing I felt tonight.

Now that I didn't have to focus on driving, I had all too much attention to focus on Gwen and the twins. I checked my link to the girls reflexively—they were fine, physically. But the spell couldn't tell me if they were scared, or what was happening to them. It couldn't tell me a thing about their mother. My chest was tight and I took a few deep breaths to calm myself. I needed to pay attention to the trail. I wasn't going to be any good to anyone if I broke my ankle.

I liked hiking—in the daytime. Navigating a trail in the woods by the beam of a flashlight was not my optimum experience. It was slow going. Unlike the road, the trail was well maintained, but it looked strange in the narrow light, all flat brights and deep shadows. Even under a full moon I couldn't have seen well enough to walk through the dark, and the moon tonight was only the barest sliver. The strap of my backpack caught in every overhanging branch, and tree roots rose up out of nowhere to trip me. The night air was cool, but I was sweating by the time I reached the crook in the trail, maybe an hour after I'd set off.

I turned the flashlight off and waited for my eyes to adjust. It was dark and quiet, except for a few late-night frogs serenading each other somewhere nearby. The trees became a barely-perceptible landscape of grays and purples. I called up my spellsight. When I first learned to see this way, it had taken minutes to achieve the necessary level of calm, but it was second nature now, as familiar and comfortable as a well-broken-in pair of boots.

A thin lattice of silver rose up, entwined throughout the forest. A botanist would have been very interested in the plants here; some of them had migrated from the other side of the gate and hybridized with local flora. But like the road in, the trail was warded against accidental wanderers, and no botanist was getting close unless he or she was also a caster. I shoved branches aside as I pushed toward the feygate. Usually foliage subtly moved to create a path, but tonight the gate was closed, and I was not welcome. At least it wasn't fighting me directly.

I broke through a net of hanging vines and around the still-mighty stump of an old oak tree, redolent of moss and decay. The feygate arched over the greenery, stonework etched with silver, glowing with far greater a light than could be accounted for by the dim moon. I had never seen it as anything other than an empty arch, but now it was emphatically closed: the arch was completely blocked. Not with a door, or a gate, but a wall of stone that could have been there for centuries. It seemed to offer no possibility of ever opening again. The silver misted in front of me. Gwen and the twins were stuck in there. The link told me the girls at least were all right, but what if they weren't? How would I get to them to keep my promise? I blinked furiously until the gate stopped shimmering.

There was a phouka at the gate in New York. Everything here seemed quiet, but I cleared my throat anyway and said "Who guards this gate?"

Nothing answered. The forest was quiet except for the occasional rustle of leaves and the distant frogs, and I had no sense of anything listening. I tried again. "Who guards this gate?" The stillness remained adamantly unbroken. Maybe there was nothing here.

Third time's the charm. "Who guards this gate?" Most minor fae couldn't resist questions asked in threes. I bit my lip when nothing answered. If this gate was unguarded, I had to move on to the next. There were several between here and Anil in Texas, and maybe one of them would be open enough to get a message to Gwen. Even just for a minute, a second, and I could—

The frogs went silent. A screech broke the night. A feathered missile flew at me from above, talons extended. I ducked, hands flying up to cover my face, and the bird came close enough to pull at my hair.

My heart hammered, and my breath came in short gasps as I scrambled to the side, hands slipping in wet moss. The smell of leaf mould rose where I had disturbed the ground cover. The silver bracelet was a heavy weight at my wrist, but I didn't want to bring out the sidheblade yet. The bird hadn't hurt me, and I'd rather talk my way out of this if I could. It might be able to help me.

The bird came around for another pass. It glowed silver in my spellsight, but I would have known this bird was unnatural even without it. Falcons weren't generally nocturnal. It called again as it circled. I pulled power from the ouroboros knot tattoo over my shoulder, channeled it into my fingertips, sketching *algiz*, a rune of protection. It wouldn't do much against a physical attack, but I hoped it would communicate my intent. The rune hung in the air, glowing and throwing off silver sparks. The falcon mantled and called again, but it sounded less strident.

"I mean you no harm." I held my hands open to show it I was weaponless. "I want to understand what's happened to the gates."

The falcon landed on a branch not far from the gate and called softly, a much more mournful sound than its previous cries. "Do you know?" I asked.

It cocked its head. A silver disc inscribed with a rowan leaf crossed by a golden arrow gleamed against its breast, hanging from a thin leather strip that circled its neck. Silk and leather jesses dangled from its legs. Some poor minor fae, most likely, bound for the entertainment of a lord. I didn't recognize the sigil. Gwen would have. My heart contracted, but I made myself focus. Even a minor fae, even bound, could hurt me badly if I were careless. I could not afford to be careless. Gwen needed me. The girls needed me. Even Eliza and the Spellcasters' Association needed me, right now.

The falcon made a strangled, croaking noise, but it wasn't attacking. It was trying to tell me something.

"I'm sorry. I don't understand."

It shook its head and hopped down the branch, closer to me. The silvery light illuminated rumpled feathers around its head and shoulders.

"Were you trying to get in the gate?"

It tilted its head until one fierce eye had me firmly in its gaze and slowly, deliberately nodded. A chill rippled my spine. "It won't open even for you?" If the gate was closed even to its own...what was happening in Faerie?

The bird just as slowly shook its head. I shivered violently, then got myself under control and bowed. It wasn't polite to thank the fae directly, but... "My name is Morgan Tenpenny. I will remember your help. If ever I can help you in return, I will." It looked straight at the closed gate, then at me. "If I thought I could open it, I would, but if the gate won't open for you, nothing I can do will work. I'm sorry I can't help more." I tilted my head respectfully and backed away, feeling my way through the trees until a trunk blocked my view of the feygate—and the falcon.

I rolled my shoulders and turned back in the direction of the road. Maybe someone had called while I was checking out the gate and I wouldn't have to do any more driving tonight.

The falcon flew past me, landed on a bush, and made a *quer-kee?* sort of noise. My shoulders tensed back up.

"I'm sorry. I can't get you in the gate."

The next noise it made was less questioning, more irritated. I hesitated, then kept walking. An annoyed squawk sounded behind me, and I drew *algiz* again and let it hang in the air. The falcon stayed silent, and after a tense moment, I hurried on. Somewhere in the woods, one of the frogs queried another, and the chorus began again.

I flicked on the flashlight but didn't let spellsight fall away. It seemed to take longer to get back to the truck than it had to reach the feygate. I was tired. Even cold, the half-cup of coffee in my truck would be welcome. "I'm too old for this," I told the woods, and the frog song didn't disagree. Forty-three was hardly decrepit, but I missed sleep more than I had in my twenties.

After what seemed like far too long, the trees opened up on the service road, where my truck was waiting. It had to be after four. The sky wasn't yet tinged with gray, but the night felt closer to morning. Adrenaline had gotten me here, but I was running on less than four hours of sleep, and it had been a long time since I pulled an all nighter. I thumbed the button on the key fob, and the truck unlocked. I could almost taste my coffee.

I tossed my tool bag into the passenger's seat and started to slide in when a scream split the silence. Heart pounding, I twisted to face the night. The falcon barreled past me and landed, mantling fiercely, on the strap of my tool bag. Its beak opened wide in a silent cry.

"What are you doing?" I yelped. "You can't come with me." I reached toward it without thinking, and the powerful beak snapped. I pulled my arm back and held both hands open, trying to look harmless. All right, then. I wasn't going to be able to remove it without a struggle, and I didn't want a struggle. I just wanted to do my damn job, check out the feygates, and find my sister.

It made a chuckling sort of noise and sidehopped closer to the window. It reached a talon to the seatbelt and tugged at it. I snorted and sat gingerly in the driver's seat. Under its glare, I buckled in. It seemed I was going to have a passenger for the rest of the night.

"Are you okay in the car?" That much steel ought to give it fits. It rolled one yellow eye and I shrugged. If it wasn't a problem, then it wasn't a problem. I wasn't completely keen on driving to the next feygate with a predator capable of taking my eyes out, but I couldn't evict it, either. And if I could figure out how to communicate with it, it might be able to shed some light on the current situation.

I took a sip of my coffee—cold but better than nothing—and was pleased my hands didn't shake. Nothing to see here—no big deal when strange fae get in my car. It was turning out to be a very odd night. I turned the key in the ignition. The truck rumbled to life and I pulled out the map and plugged the charmingly-named Bogue Chitto state park, one of the newest feygates, into my GPS, which told me I had a little over a six hour drive. At least after a while it'd be light. The falcon tilted its head, looked at the map, and made a slight, derisive noise. I ignored it and set off down the gravel service road.

Once we were on the highway I dialed Eliza, who picked up after the first ring. "Yeah?"

"Nothing. The first gate was shut solid. Not a clue how or why."

"This one too. Any word from anyone else?"

"Anil's checking the gate in Texas. I'm on my way to Louisiana. No one else has called."

"We have another problem." Another fae trapped on the wrong side of a gate? I glanced sideways at the falcon, who was listening. I decided not to mention it to Eliza until later. She would want to know, but she wasn't the one sitting next to it if it got pissed off I told her about it. "Seth is sick." It took me a minute to remember who Seth was. Seth. The spellcaster who lived near a gate in Georgia, near Magnolia Springs.

"What's wrong with him?"

"I don't know. It's not something I've seen before. But it's...somehow, it's twisted up all the lines of energy in his body."

"Are you saying he has some kind of magic flu?" I heard the incredulity in my own voice, but I couldn't help it. It was ridiculous. "A metaphysical sickness?"

"I don't know," Eliza snapped. Then, "Sorry. I'm on edge." *And you haven't slept any more than I have.* "I've called in Dr. Ramachandran. She's on her way here." Saranya Ramachandran worked at the Center for Disease Control. She was also one of the casters I'd left a message for. If she was on a plane from Atlanta to New York, at least I knew why she hadn't called back.

"Let me know what she says. I haven't heard from anyone else. I'm going to stop by Helen Oshiro's since she's on the way to the next gate."

"All right. We'll keep in touch."

"Yes." A reassurance for both of us that we wouldn't be the people not answering our phones, as if we could guarantee it. I hung up without saying goodbye and dropped my cell into the cup holder next to the travel mug.

The sky lightened behind us as the highway rolled by. After the third time I yawned I started looking for a McDonald's or Starbucks along the exits. For a few moments, the sky was gray, and then after that it paled, dawn pressing in, a visible reminder of my lack of sleep, and then a pink sliver of the sun was over the horizon and rising. Despite everything, the daylight lifted my mood.

"Well, maybe it's not so—" I turned to the fae in the

passenger seat, and almost swallowed my tongue. One moment, the falcon had been a small brown shadow out of the corner of my eye, and now, as the first light of dawn struck, it blurred, and resolved into a naked man.

"Morgan," he croaked, and I heard the falcon in his voice. I straight armed the wheel to keep myself from running us off the road.

"How—? What—?" I said, like any callow caster who'd never run into the fae before. Some of them wore curses tied to the sun or the moon, or the love of someone who'd died centuries before, and they liked to toss them onto mortals who crossed their paths. There was almost always some loophole, some out, but it was never anything you'd want to do. I didn't want this fae passing his curse on to me.

"Please." He coughed. "A moment."

I tried to keep my eyes on the road. The man next to me was handsome and well-built as all the fae court were, naked but for the leather cord and the silver medallion crossed with gold around his neck, but as the sun rose above trees and cloud formations, his shadow seemed edged with the suggestion of feathers. Gwen would have known the sigil and known who cursed him. Gwen might have known him by sight. There were a thousand subtle markers that would have told her how to interact with him. I would have to parse it out through conversation.

"I beg your pardon, lady." He coughed again. "I owe you a debt for taking me with you. Perhaps together we can find a way back underhill."

"Do you know why the gates shut, lord..." Was he actually a lord of the fae court or only a minor fae, as I'd thought before? Safer to err on the side of caution. Being overly polite never hurt anyone. Being rude, even accidentally, could.

"You may call me Falcon. It's probably best for the both of us."

"All right, lord Falcon." *If that is your real name*—which it most certainly wasn't. I glanced at him, which was a mistake. There was nothing feathery about his silhouette now, and he wore nothing besides the medallion at his neck. *The fae are not embarrassed by nudity,* I told myself, *and neither am I.* But it was hard not to look.

He did not seem much taller than me. His hair was the same color as the falcon's wings, and fell about his shoulders in a tangle. The medallion glinted in the hollow between his collarbones. *He looks younger than me; he's probably older than my great grandfather.*

I had to focus. Now that he could talk, he might be able to tell me something, and I was wasting time being flustered. "Take a look in the back. There might be a jacket or something you can put on behind your seat." A towel, even, would be welcome.

"A jacket?" He looked down. "Ah. Indeed. The gesture is appreciated, but unnecessary." Light shifted next to me. He had conjured clothes, and they weren't the overly formal, archaic court clothes I'd seen Elm and his family wear, but jeans, boots, and a t-shirt. *A glamour, not real clothes.* Still, it was less distracting and he wouldn't get arrested for public indecency.

"What happened with the gates?"

"I am uncertain."

I bit back a frustrated response. We both wanted to know. *We want the same thing, for now*. It might not make us allies, exactly, but as long as we both wanted to find out why the feygates had closed, we could help each other. I just needed to be careful.

He tapped long fingers together, thinking. "I felt the queen's summons, but I waited too long in the woods." Some twist in his voice suggested there was more to it. "Something rippled down the leylines, and I did hurry then, but I was too slow. The wall filled the gate all in an instant, and I could not pass, though the summons still called me. You are certain no human magic can...?"

"None that I know of." When I got back home, I'd check the library I'd accumulated throughout my career as a caster for any references to alternate routes to Faerie, or the gates closing in the past, but I didn't remember anything off the top of my head. "Do you know why the queen summoned you?"

"I do not think it was a summons meant particularly for me—it was too impersonal for that. I think she meant all those who visit the upper lands to return to Faerie." He sighed and leaned his head against the window.

"I doubt you're the only one." He glanced back at me. "A colleague north of here tells me at least one gate is guarded by a phouka."

"Well," he murmured. "Indeed. And who else might await us?" The thought seemed to brighten him a little.

My phone rang. The number was unknown, but I answered anyway. "This is Morgan." Falcon watched curiously.

Static crackled down the line, but nothing else. Hairs prickled along my arms. "Hello?"

"Morgan....I need your help..." The voice was male, and familiar, but tenuous with distance and I couldn't immediately place it.

"Who is this?"

A choking laugh. "It's Marcus."

"Where are you?" I put the blinker on and pulled onto the side of the road. Almost running off the highway twice in an hour wasn't on my agenda today. My body felt cold and still with shock. I hadn't spoken to my mentor, much less seen him, in eighteen years. After Matthew's disastrous stunt, Marcus Grey had stopped taking students and dropped out of the network of spellcasters entirely. Eliza and I had speculated many times that he was dead because it was almost preferable to his being alive and rejecting us so thoroughly.

The sound of his voice, even distant and staticky, woke a confusion of emotions in me: relief, joy, anger...and even the student's eagerness to please that I thought I'd outgrown twenty years ago.

I retreated in my own way, moving to a small town where no one knew me and I'd always be an outsider, but I hadn't disappeared as he had. I was still helping Eliza and the Association, still helping the people around me. The man who had taught me the responsibility a caster has to her community had gotten in touch precisely once after the mess with Matthew, and that was right now.

"Strange...hold..." A burst of white noise interrupted

him and I wasn't sure if I'd heard him right. The phrase rang a vague bell, but nothing solid. A person? A place? A jiu-jitsu move? I couldn't bring it to the tip of my brain.

"Marcus...What? Where are you? Give me something more."

Distant, tinny static.

"Marcus! Hello? Are you there?"

The line went dead.

"Damn it!" I beat the steering wheel in frustration and tried to redial the number, but it went straight to a busy signal.

My passenger cleared his throat delicately. I had almost forgotten he was there, which was suicidally stupid around the fae. "Your caller...Was that Marcus Grey?"

I managed to keep my mouth from dropping open, barely. "You've heard of him?"

"Indeed I have." His smile was sharp, edged. "I have been in the mortal realm a long time, Morgan. Marcus and I worked together, decades ago." He shot me a sidelong look that I couldn't interpret. If Marcus had mentioned him, I didn't remember, or he had spoken of him with a different name.

"I haven't seen him in almost twenty years." Would my passenger have heard of what Matthew did? Doubtless. *Everyone* had heard of Matthew. He had nearly ended the truce between our peoples. "But I don't know where he is, or how I can help him. And the feygates are still shut. My friend in New York tells me another of our people is sick. But not just sick—somehow it's affecting him magically."

Falcon looked at me without comment. He was fae,

not human; maybe the fae had magical sicknesses all the time. I'd have to ask Gwen, if I could. There was so much going wrong. A pulse of panic brought bile to the back of my throat. How could I possibly do everything I needed to do? I checked the link to my nieces for the umpteenth time since the gates had closed. It was still there, cobweb-thin but undisturbed. They were still okay.

"You are fatigued," Falcon observed.

"Yes, tha—I do appreciate your noticing." I refrained from rubbing the corners of my eyes. We were still in Alabama. I didn't think I could make it to Louisiana without a break.

"You should rest before your abilities become compromised."

"I will. After we check on Helen."

He hesitated. "I am fatigued as well."

"After Helen," I said, "we will rest."

He nodded, not as if he were pleased, but it wasn't far to Helen's. I called her again with no better result than any of the other times. She'd answer if she could. I tried not to think of all the possible reasons she couldn't.

The sun was well up and my eyelids felt like someone had stapled weights to them by the time I pulled up in front of Helen's house. It was the house her children had grown up in; she had not moved once they were grown and gone, and not when her husband had died.

"All right," I told Falcon. "Let's see what's going on, and then we'll find a place to rest." He nodded, frowning, and stared at the house. I followed his gaze, but couldn't tell what was bothering him. "Are you okay? Is something wrong?"

"I...am well. But this place...the wards..."

Well, that told me nothing solid and raised hairs down my arms. I took a breath and summoned my spellsight. A net of fading silver draped around the house—Helen's wards, in the looping swirls that I associated with her casting—with a black hole in the middle of it like a cigarette burn in a wedding veil. A shudder rippled the skin on my back. There were only a few reasons her wards might be fading, none of them good. And I'd never seen anything like that hole.

We walked to the door and I leaned on the doorbell. Helen lived alone; there was no one I could bother, unless she had guests, and if her guests were keeping her from answering the phone I was happy to bother them. No one answered, and I heard nothing.

The door was locked, but I was a spellcaster. I pulled energy from the ouroboros tattoo at my shoulder and forced the lock. This was crude magic, simple application of force to create a "key," with none of the elegance of the spells Marcus had taught us, but it was also much faster, with much less in the way of set up. Falcon watched, frowning, but said nothing.

The door swung open and I stepped into the dark front hallway. It smelled wrong. Helen was a meticulous housekeeper, much more so than I, and there was a faint scent of vomit underlying that of cleaning products and air freshener. I called her name a few times, but there was no answer, so I went deeper into the house, Falcon at my shoulder. It was a split-level, with her kitchen, living room, and office on the first floor, and a den a level down—all empty. The stairs creaked as I went up them; they were silent under Falcon's feet, and I focused on my annoyance at typical fae ubercompetence rather than the unease dogging me through Helen's silent house. I stopped at the hall bathroom. The smell of vomit was stronger. I braced myself.

"Helen?" No answer. I pushed the door open, then took a step back, swallowing hard.

She was leaning against the wall across from the toilet as though resting, but her eyes were wide and staring and she looked—well. I ran to check her pulse to be sure, but I already knew.

"Back away," Falcon said from the hallway. "Stop touching her and back away."

I let my fingers slide away from her wrist and did as he said. "What is it?" I had to clear my throat before my voice was steady. After two decades of working together, she had been more than an ally. Most spellcasters felt a bit like family simply because we all shared the same secret—some of them the weird dysfunctional family that you wanted to avoid, to be sure—but Helen had been a friend as well. Not the first friend I'd lost, but it didn't get easier. Each grief added up, took a little more sunshine out of the world.

"Look at her." I glanced back at her body, but I saw nothing. "No. Use your sorcerer's sight."

His voice was sharp, so I did as he suggested rather than inform him that no one said sorcerer anymore. Silver veiled my vision, surrounded by the slowly-dissolving wards and enchantments that had run through Helen's home. Reluctantly, I returned my gaze to Helen.

And sucked in air. Her magic should have been fading like her wards, the silver strands dimming and falling apart, but hers were still bright and moving, knotting more tightly about her. They looked like worms sinking into her dead skin, and I flinched back reflexively, swallowing hard to keep my coffee from coming back up my throat. She was my friend, and she was being eaten by the magic she had mastered. Bile burned the back of my throat.

"What is it?" I couldn't keep revulsion from my voice.

"It's nothing I've ever seen. Might I suggest we leave this house?"

A glint of metal against the tile floor caught my eye. A bracelet. Helen hadn't gone in for tattoos as I did—not many casters did; you could get a lot of power from them, but it could be dangerous to hold that much magic next to your skin all the time, and if something went wrong it was right there *on* you—so like many folks, she wore wards and spells in jewelry. Among a number of silver charms, there were three spheres of clear quartz, clouded and shot through with cracks. I scooped up the bracelet with one finger and shoved it into my pocket, then beat a retreat out of the room.

The worms of Helen's power surged above her skin and sank back down into it. I was only too happy to take his suggestion—and, I noted, his voice had wavered as well. Whatever scared a fae into audibly losing control was something I didn't want to deal with.

Unfortunately, I didn't see a whole lot of other options.

I slammed the door behind us as we tumbled out onto the front porch—more like children who'd been dared into a witch's house than like a veteran spellcaster and a fae whatever-he-was. My chest was heaving and sweat cooled the small of my back. Falcon looked none too sanguine either, which was some small consolation. I took out my phone. Falcon shot me a look I couldn't quite interpret, so I held up a finger in the universal signal for *just a second.* The fae had so many more years than the rest of us, there was a real possibility that to him it meant *wait a month*, but he waited and didn't tap his foot or vanish into nothing. With the feygates shut, maybe he couldn't.

Eliza picked up after the fourth ring, right when I was sure it was about to go to voice mail. "Yes?"

"Helen's dead." I took a breath to keep my voice steady. "It's weird. There are spell lines around her body when she's clearly gone. All her wards are dissolving, but the magic is still doing something. I don't like it at all. I'm going to cast a ward around her house until Dr. Ramachandran can get a look at her."

"Morgan...have you turned on the news at all?"

A retort almost made it past my lips, but I bit it back and came up with something more measured. "I've been a little busy, to be honest. Did you not hear me that Helen is dead?"

"Morgan..." It was bad if she was calling me by name this much. "...She's not the only one. A lot of people are very sick."

My stomach dropped. "Is it...?"

I didn't even know what I was asking, but she had an

answer to the question I couldn't formulate. "Casters are getting sick, Morgan. Lots of us. Even the mundane world has noticed. Be careful." Something hit the phone and I heard a muffled cough. She had put her hand over it to quiet it.

"You be careful, too, Eliza." Ice curdled my gut at the thought of her like Helen, wormed through by her own magic.

"Cast the ward. Saranya will come or—or—someone will." She coughed again.

"Eliza—"

"I'll talk to you tomorrow. Maybe I'll have something better to tell you."

"Tomorrow." I only said it so I wouldn't have to say goodbye. I ended the call with a feeling of all-too-specific dread.

Falcon was standing a few feet away, arms crossed. "I have to ward this," I told him. "Whatever that was, we can't leave it where anyone might stumble in and touch those—those worms."

His mouth twisted, but he nodded. "I'll help."

My eyebrows shot up, but I managed to keep from blurting out anything stupid in my surprise. The fae and mortal spellcasters had been in a state of uneasy détente for decades now, more likely to circle each other warily than offer aid. But then again, the feygates were shut and something nasty was happening, so if there were ever a time for cooperation, this was it. "I'd appreciate that. My thought was to cast a circle with salt and stone, rowan and ash." And yes, salt and stone were both rocks, but salt affected magic differently than other crystals did. If we were casting a circle inside, I might have gone with just salt, not stone, but I wanted something more permanent, that couldn't be washed away—although it meant it would take longer, and I was so tired. But if Falcon truly meant to help me...

His lips twisted in a faint smile and he nodded thoughtfully. "I'll add my power to yours."

It was a generous offer. I'd never cast with a fae before—I didn't know anyone who had, besides possibly Gwen; maybe someday things would be easy enough between both lands to share knowledge freely, but the time wasn't yet—and I wasn't sure what to expect. Human magic was relatively slow and ponderous, and required set up. I used props, like salt or circles or incense, to alter the flow of magic, or sifted and stored it in my tattoos—an arduous process, but one that allowed me to perform some kinds of spells more quickly. The fae worked with glamours and curses, mostly, and their methods were quicker and more intuitive than the ones we used, as far as I knew, anyway. There could be a school for fae magic underhill, and how the hell would anyone know about it?

Gwen might. The girls might.

I shoved them out of my head with an effort and went to the truck to get my tool bag. Falcon followed behind me, casting an uneasy look over his shoulder at the house. A few weeks back I had cleared out a half-full bag of river stones I'd used in a garden project; a shame, because they would have been useful now. But I never went anywhere without salt—there was a small Ziploc bag of kosher salt in my tool kit, and a forty-pound bag of extra coarse in my truck bed. Crystals held spells particularly well, like the quartz on Helen's bracelet, and salt had other properties that made it useful. It both held spells and could break them. I grunted as I lifted the cooler that I kept the salt in and dropped it to the ground. I opened the cooler and ripped open the bag, pulling out a handful of salt crystals to show Falcon. They were bigger than table salt, the size of small pebbles themselves.

The house wasn't too big, but my back ached before we made it halfway around. I scattered herbs mixed with chips of ash and rowan, and then followed it with chunks of salt. All the while I was coaxing magic stored in my ouroboros knot tattoo to follow the spell, encouraging the various rocks and pebbles that lay on Helen's property to join with the ward. A faint trace of silver showed when we made our way back to the beginning. We walked three times around and when we overlapped our footsteps the final time, silver soared up into a dome around Helen's house. Even if her sons came to the house, they would turn away, forgetting why they were there in the first place.

Her daughter was another matter; she was a caster herself. I would have to call her. Someone had to tell her that her mother was dead, and as far I could see, that person was me. I swallowed again and turned to Falcon. It hadn't been too different, working with him. Now all that was left was to tap the leyline and write the rune to seal the circle, and we were done. "I appreciate your help," I began, but he shook his head, eyebrows drawing together.

"Wait." He turned back toward the house. I listened, but I couldn't tell what had caught his attention. He stepped carefully across the circle we'd made and headed for the back door. The silver wall rippled around him, as yet unsealed. I watched, frowning, as he bent to the door and listened for a second, then straightened and yanked the door open.

A little poodle-y spaniel-type dog spilled out the door and down the steps. Its tail wagged furiously and it looked up at Falcon like he was its savior. He bent down and rubbed its ears as it ducked and barked frantically around him. I dug in my backpack and found a half-empty packet of jerky, and walked over to the fae and the dog.

"I forgot Helen had a dog." I'd never seen it for very long before she put it in the laundry room if there were people coming over. Now I couldn't remember its name. Biscuit? Cookie? Something food-related.

"The poor creature will hardly know what to do with itself with no mistress to serve," Falcon said. I leaned down and fed it jerky, which disappeared in seconds. How long had it been locked in the laundry room waiting for Helen to let it out? My throat tightened with grief I'd been too freaked out to feel when confronted by her body.

I coughed. "I've got more jerky in the car. The back yard is fenced in. I'll let Helen's daughter know the dog is here when I call her."

He looked at me thoughtfully, then bent down and spoke to the dog in a fae language. Which one, I didn't know; I spoke a few words of High Court, but I didn't recognize this. The dog barked back. Falcon gestured a spell out of the air, but I couldn't tell what it was.

"He will wait in the back yard," Falcon said.

"What did you do?"

"If his new masters are unsatisfactory, he may come to Faerie. I have shown him a way to get there, once the gates are open again."

"He understood about feygates and underhill?"

"He understood enough to have a choice."

I nodded, accepting it. The dog leaned against my leg, tail wagging furiously. I opened the gate to the fenced-in back yard and let him in, dumping out another pack of jerky for him. One we were back outside the circle, it was time to seal the ward.

"All right," I said. "Let's get this done." I pulled the silver energy of the dome together, closing the place where we'd walked through it, and drew a rune of warning to communicate my intent. It was as solid as I could make it now, and I started to reach for the ley energy to bolster my strength. But Falcon wasn't done.

He took my hand, turned to the silver dome, and *spoke* to it.

Magic is stronger in Faerie, or more pervasive, anyway. There are no thin spots like there are here, no danger of running out of power. As Marcus explained it to me, magic comes from the space between our world and Faerie, leaking in from between the worlds. There are other worlds, it's been theorized, hanging next to each other like pearls on a string, touching but not overlapping. Faerie is the closest one, and smaller than us. Unlike here, where magic is spread relatively thinly over the earth, there it saturates everything. That's why the fae and even their landscape are so mutable, and why there are stories of people going underhill and coming back a hundred years later.

Here, you have to seek it out. There, it's everywhere. It soaks into the land, the people, the food, the air, so the way the fae interact with it is different than the way casters here do. I couldn't tell how Falcon pulled the energy to him, but it wasn't how I'd have brought it from the leyline. He turned to me, and it was there.

And then he sent it to me.

The silver flared brighter, and I felt his magic in my bones, curling through me. It lingered in the sigils graved on my skin, a long touch wilder than magic from leylines, and I sent it effortlessly into the ward we'd cast, amplifying it and shaping it. The power and the unexpectedly intimate feel of it melding with my own efforts shut my mouth entirely, and when he turned to me, his eyes were wild and vivid, new-leaf green. His chest heaved as he sucked in breath; I felt as though I'd run a race myself.

He was beautiful and the power he'd just shared with me was intoxicating, but I had never been more aware of the danger he posed. Magically speaking, he could crush me like an ant.

"This will keep it," he told me. "No one will enter."

*

I got us two rooms at a Motel 6 off I-20. I spent the first few minutes alone composing a quick email to my clients letting them know I'd be gone a few days for a family emergency, and then braced myself. After I called Helen's daughter to tell her about her mother and the dog—and what a fun conversation that was—I hopped in the shower. I was too wired to skip it, even as exhausted as I was. I combed my hair in the green fluorescent bathroom light and coughed experimentally in the steamy air. My throat didn't hurt. I was just so very tired.

But as tired as I was, I couldn't sleep. Not yet. I turned on the TV and flicked through channels until I found a news station. The anchors couldn't maintain their composure. "Dozens dead...airports closed...the president has declared a state of emergency...officials ask that residents stay in their homes...CDC officials report that they have not yet isolated the vector..." They were calling it the Savannah flu because patient zero had been hospitalized at St. Joseph's in Savannah, Georgia, but Savannah was a port city, if I recalled. It could have come from anywhere. Something about Savannah dinged a bell in some distant recess of my mind. If only I hadn't been so tired...

I fell asleep with images of hospital rooms flashing behind my eyelids, a meld of old memories and current events. I didn't sleep well.

A knock on the door woke me. It was unlikely to be anyone but Falcon, but my pulse knocked against my temples. I readied a protective spell with energy from the ouroboros tattooed on my shoulder just in case, and kept it armed and ready as I opened the door. It was indeed Falcon, so I let the magic fizzle back to my tattoo.

"It lacks only a few hours until sundown," he said. "I thought we might get something to eat before the sun sets."

For a long stupid moment, I just stared at him, until I remembered him shifting in the cab of my truck at sunrise. When the sun went down, he'd shift back. "Oh. Of course." I longed to know the nature of his curse, but fae or not, I couldn't help but feel it would be the height of rudeness to outright ask him.

"I will not be as much use to you in the night, but nor will I be entirely worthless." He smiled grimly.

I hesitated. Did he know how to use a TV? "Did you see the news?" I grabbed my bag and the key to the room. This motel was so out-of-date it was an actual metal key, not a card.

He nodded, his face shadowed. "It's bad."

"Very, very bad." Understatement of the year. I sent a wave of energy through the tattoo over my heart to the girls. They were alive. I had to hope they were safe. His gaze sharpened.

"Do you have a—"

What he wanted to ask, I never found out. The mirror over the couch swirled frantically, and Gwen's face resolved in a blur of color. She was standing in what I assumed was her bedroom at the Faerie court, a baroque but elegant fantasy of silk and curved, gilded wood.

"Morgan! I've been trying to reach you for days!"

"Gwen!" I ran to the mirror and only barely stopped myself from touching the frame as if it were her hand. If I disrupted the spell, when she was reaching out to me... "What's happening? Why are the feygates closed?"

"The queen closed them," she said shortly. "It seems her suspicions were right. Someone—someone human—tried to launch some kind of attack on the court. She repulsed it, but it was close enough to successful that she..." She glanced to the side, then back at the mirror. "She had a lot of questions for me. I don't know how long I'll be safe here, Morgan. And the twins..."

"Is there anywhere you can go underhill?"

Gwen's eyebrows lifted then drew together. "I want to bring them to you."

I shook my head helplessly. "It's not safe for them here either." I filled her in on the Savannah flu. "And it's attacking casters, not regular people. Helen's dead, and Eliza didn't sound that great last time I talked to her. Don't bring the girls here, Gwen. If you can hold out there—if Elm can help you—I saw Helen. It's not anything you want happening to you, much less the girls."

Her eyes flicked from side to side, but she nodded. "Remember your promise."

"Don't talk like that. There won't be any need." She glared, and I put my hand over my heart. "I swore. I won't forget." Her shoulders sagged fractionally, and in that movement I read all the fear she wouldn't express. The image rippled. That she had held it this long through the closed gates was impressive enough.

"Find me. Let me know when it's safe. I don't know how long we'll have and the queen—" The mirror flickered one more time and was still, reflecting only my ashen, worried face, the bland hotel room, and Falcon, watching me.

*

"So the human ambassador to Faerie..." Falcon dipped a French fry in ketchup and stared at it dubiously.

"Is my sister," I finished. I rolled a bottled beer back and forth between my hands. The cool glass felt good. I knew I needed to eat—should be ravenous, in fact, since all I'd had all day was a granola bar and some jerky—but a cold knot had settled in my stomach, and the turkey sandwich and fries didn't look all that appetizing. The TV in the corner of the bar wasn't helping. Even though the sound was muted, images flashed across the screen—bodies wrapped in shrouds, medical staff in masks, EMTs in hazmat suits. They still weren't sure of the vector of transmission. The restaurant was almost empty except for us, and the servers watched us with wary eyes.

"Then I know your brother-in-law." Falcon's smile had an odd edge to it. Some history there. How big was the fae court? Would he know everyone? They lived a long time, collecting grudges like charms on a bracelet as near as I could tell.

"Then you know more than I. I've only met him a few times." A few highly awkward times. Gwen wasn't supposed to fall in love at court, she was supposed to represent human interests in Faerie and help preserve the fragile peace one of her predecessors had brokered forty years before. An alliance by marriage was a traditional form among the fae and we could have made use of it, but Gwen had chosen with her heart, not her head. It was unlike her, to say the least. Her entire career had been a slow, calculated climb to her current position—whereas mine was a tangle guided by necessity more than a plan, full of detours driven by disaster. I sipped my beer, letting the dark flavor coat my tongue. None of that mattered now.

"He's a good man." Falcon hesitated. "Perhaps not the most political." No, Gwen had not used her head. I forced myself to take a bite of my sandwich.

"Will they be safe there?"

He took a long swallow of his own beer. "No one's ever safe anywhere."

Well, that was reassuring. I let it go for the moment. "We have several problems." I held up a hand and ticked them off on my fingers. "This Savannah flu, whatever it is—I need to call Dr. Ramachandran and see what she's found out. The queen has shut the gates because someone tried to attack her, or maybe Faerie itself. Someone will know who and what they did. In the meantime, Gwen and the girls are stuck underhill, and you're stuck here. If there's a way through—there's still this sickness. And Marcus is somewhere, and he needs help. Does 'Strange hold' mean anything to you?"

"Strangehold? That's a name I've heard only in whispers." He took another swig of his beer, looking at the glass with far more approval than he had the food.

I allowed myself cautious optimism. "Marcus said something about it when he called."

Falcon nodded. "A friend of mine went there—when she came back, she would only speak of it obliquely, and only after I swore never to speak of it to any of the Shining Court. From what I understand, it's an old back way between underhill and over."

A cautious tendril of hope stirred. Another route to Faerie? Maybe I could get to Gwen and the girls. "A back way?"

"My friend told me there were doors to it here and there." He drew a squiggle in the condensation from his beer. It glowed faintly and branched into much narrower, finer lines. They split and rejoined, meandering across the tabletop, and I realized I was looking at a map. Falcon frowned in concentration, his eyes distant. "Here, I think, and here..." One in New York, it looked like, and one in D.C. He frowned. "But the closest would be...Ah." The lines squirmed and rearranged themselves. "Atlanta." He looked at me, pleased.

"These seem like awfully urban areas for a back door to underhill."

"I believe part of the point was to put them somewhere a lord or lady of the high court would be uncomfortable going." That crooked smile again.

"Do you think you could get us there?"

He looked at me. "Were we not going to the next feygate?"

"We were." I bit the inside of my lip. Eliza would be pissed. Things were falling apart here and I shouldn't leave. But then again...maybe she wouldn't. If I told her Marcus had asked... "I'll call Anil and get him to check the gate in Louisiana. If we can really find another way to Faerie—"

"I'll get in touch with my friend and see what else she can tell me."

"Can you do that with the gates closed? It was hard for Gwen to get through to me."

He ran a finger through his map, and it was only water droplets again. "In this case, I'll rely on sympathetic magic. I have something that once belonged to the lady. That should be enough to let me reach her."

My mind buzzed with speculation. The only thing he seemed to carry through his transformation was the metal disc and the chain it hung on. Was his friend the person who'd cursed him? He was frowning at the water and I didn't ask. I pulled at my beer and made myself pick the sandwich up again. "All right. We'll head there tomorrow."

He looked up, but his eyes were still distant. "And what will we find?"

*

We left early and hit Atlanta before lunch hour traffic got too bad. I had steeled myself and called Eliza, but she didn't answer. I squelched worry and left a message telling her Marcus had sent me on a lead, and I'd asked Anil to check up on the Bogue Chitto gate. I said not to worry if she couldn't get in touch, because I might be out of cell range, but I was okay. I hoped I wasn't lying.

Someone had a sense of humor; the backdoor to underhill was in Underground Atlanta. Someone had affixed three two-by-four planks of wood to the bricked walls in a rough arch with a ward that would keep most eyes from noticing it. The wood was weathered and splintering, and I couldn't find any screws or nails. When I looked with spellsight, silvery strands threaded through the wood. It was not as strong nor as obvious as a feygate, and I doubted I'd have been able to sense it from even a street away.

"So tell me how this works." Trusting myself to a feygate was one thing; they were established and had been around for centuries, even millennia, some of them. This rickety thing was some stranger's spell, and I had no way of knowing how skilled a caster they were.

"It doesn't go directly to Faerie—Strangehold is between our worlds."

I raised an eyebrow. Someone had built a way

through...what? The space between worlds? The thought made my head hurt. "That seems..." Impossible? Improbable, certainly. "...unlikely."

"According to my friend, this door leads to Strangehold, and there'll be a door to Faerie somewhere inside."

"Who made it? A fae, or a human caster?"

He shrugged. "Briar didn't know, or didn't tell me. All I can tell is that whoever did it was a Tolkien nerd."

I looked at him blankly.

He laid a hand on the wood and whispered, "*Mellon*."

"What?"

"'Speak friend, and enter.'" I looked at him blankly. "*Mellon* means *friend* in elvish. Have you never read *Lord of the Rings*?"

"I haven't even seen the movies." So Falcon was a Tolkien nerd himself. I had no room to judge—my parents were Arthurian nerds, and I had picked up a lot of it by osmosis, or in self defense. But all I knew of Tolkien was what I'd picked up from people talking about the movies. I'd been too worried about what the actual fae were doing to want to see imaginary elves. The silvery threads in the wood expanded and met, twining around each other, weaving across the arch until it gleamed like a mirror, but reflected nothing. Falcon waved a gracious hand indicating I should precede him. I told myself not to be a coward, and stepped through.

The silver clung to me as I walked through it, but it felt like the comforting hand of a friend against my skin; nothing malignant, nothing so powerful as a feygate, or as breathtakingly pervasive as Falcon's magic. Then I was through.

Strangehold was a hold indeed; it looked like some bastard child of a fortress and a luxury tree house, set inside a vast and echoing twilight void. If it was a cavern, I could see no walls. A tree trunk wider around than a football field rose from murky, unknowable, and possibly Stygian depths, wreathed with leafy vines. I could just make out a staircase spiraling around and around the trunk as it sank into the gloom. A narrow bridge apparently made of woven vines crossed the vast chasm from where I stood, which was an all-too-small platform of wooden planks, thankfully sturdier than the arch on the other side of the door had been. I wasn't prone to vertigo or fear of heights, but the depths the little bridge spanned were breathtaking. I looked down once and decided once was one time too many. At irregular intervals around the cavern, there were other platforms floating in the air (realizing ours was also floating over nothing made my stomach lurch), other rickety walkways over the void. They all converged on the building.

The structure on the other side of the bridge was a castle set into and around the tree trunk. Stone and wood melded and worked with each other, imposing walls broken by graceful arched windows. Vines grew over and around the walls, but they seemed to support the walls rather than pull them apart. It was fantastical.

But no less fantastical was the amount of magic surging around me. I didn't have to summon my caster's sight to see it; indeed, I was afraid I might blind myself if I tried. It was like standing under a waterfall, when I was used to a slow moving river. It pounded against my skin and I clutched the thin wooden railing in front of me to steady myself while I acclimated to the force of it.

The arch shimmered behind me, and Falcon stepped through. He straightened and took a deep breath. Some tension I hadn't been aware he was carrying melted away from him. "Worried we wouldn't make it?"

He glanced at me and raised an eyebrow. "What? No, not at all. But it seems Strangehold is free from outside influence." My face must have been blank. He smiled. "I am not bound to change with the sun." Interesting—whatever curse he was carrying worked overhill, and, I presumed, in Faerie, but not here...wherever here was. Perhaps because there was no sun? I looked up. The tree went up and up, the staircase spiraling around. Vast branches split off above us. It seemed to get a little lighter, a silver light tinged with the green of the foliage, that might or might not have been some kind of sunlight.

"What's up with the bridges? They seem...unnecessarily flimsy."

"No one could ever bring an army here. Not easily, anyway. Shall we?"

He held out his arm. I slid my hand into the crook of it, told myself not to look down again, and stepped forward.

The walkway swayed alarmingly, and I hissed in apprehension. "It's all right," Falcon said. Vines snaked up from the base of the bridge, so fast that before I had the chance to be alarmed, they had formed a rail at waist height. Greenery raveled before us, the railing stretching all the way across the bridge. A chill iced the skin down my spine. The amount of magic necessary to make this place was mindboggling; maybe they'd *had* to build it here, because otherwise even in Faerie there wouldn't be enough to support it. Did it respond on its own to our presence? Or was there a caster here, somewhere, watching us? My hand tightened on Falcon's arm involuntarily. I didn't know whether that was a good idea. He had been nothing but helpful so far, but he was fae. It wasn't that they were inherently untrustworthy—though some people thought so—but they had their own agendas, which were not always comprehensible to humans. Our paths pointed the same way at the moment, but there was no guarantee that they would continue to do so, especially if the way to Faerie from Strangehold allowed him home.

Crossing the swaying, bouncing bridge was no fun, even with the railing. My stomach was in knots by the time we reached the other end and my shoulders tight and creeping toward my ears. Falcon looked as calm and at ease as when we started across. If he was amused by my discomfiture, he didn't let it show.

The bridge terminated in a landing on the vast staircase winding round the trunk of the tree. The staircase continued another quarter-rotation until it widened into a courtyard. From here I could just make out twisted cypresses flanking double doors. We started off toward it, up the staircase.

The tree trunk we walked by was pierced with more of the windows I had seen from across the bridge. Some were set with faceted glass, some with colored panels, and some with undecorated panes, but even where the glass was clear, I couldn't see inside, only the reflection of the eerie cavern around us. My legs ached from walking up steps by the time we reached the courtyard.

The double doors swung open at our approach. Gravel crunched beneath my feet as we crossed the courtyard. A floral smell drifted from potted flowering trees. Inside, the floor was warm, polished hardwood of different colors laid in a pattern; if it was meant to suggest anything other than pleasing symmetry, I couldn't see it. We entered, and the doors swung shut behind us with an unfortunately final sound.

A grand double staircase was dimly visible across a vast, unlit room at the end of the entrance hall, and numerous doors flanked the hallway itself. The place was quiet, not a ticking clock or distant teakettle to break the silence. "If Marcus is here, how will we find him?" My voice bounced hollowly off the walls and the beautiful wooden floor.

Falcon shrugged. "I suppose we'll just have to look." He cupped his hands around his mouth and called "Marcus Grey!" Echoes rang through the empty hallway, dispersing and falling away into nothingness.

I pulled open a door at random. A coat closet. Kind of prosaic for a place like this. The next revealed a sitting room with an escritoire in a corner. I didn't really expect Marcus to be sitting in a room right by the doorway.

Falcon looked at me and shrugged again.

As we reached the end of the hall, I thought I heard

something beyond the small noises of our movements. I put my hand on his arm to check him. He cocked his head and his mouth thinned. Footsteps. Someone was coming down the grand staircase. The sidheblade rested in the silver bracelet at my wrist. I had not needed to draw it, and I wouldn't except in dire need, out of consideration for my companion. But it was comforting to know it was there.

Lights flickered into being as a figure walked down the staircase. As she came closer, I saw a delicate fae woman—I couldn't help thinking "maiden"—in an elegant silver dress, white-blonde hair cascading down her back, one hand on the wooden railing. She looked carved from moonlight, but I didn't trust it. The fae were rarely as fragile as they seemed.

Falcon dropped to one knee as she came to the bottom of the steps. "Lady Hawthorn." Surprise threaded his voice—and possibly, dismay? Or was I reading too much into two words? "I didn't know—that is to say, I am surprised to see you here."

"You should be, since I have taken great pains to conceal myself. I am most wroth you have found me." She lifted her chin and glared at him. Her eyes glowed like amethyst in sunshine. How could Gwen possibly live with people like this? Maybe one grew used to such unearthly beauty. "Are you here on the queen's command?"

"No, lady. I truly am surprised to see you. I've come on another errand."

Relief washed across her lovely face. "If I am not to die today, Lord Rowan, then I will be happy to help you. What do you seek?"

Wait, what?

"I no longer serve as her majesty's Blade," he said shortly. "I have not for nigh on twenty years."

Hair stood up on my arms and I found myself rubbing the bracelet where my sidheblade was hidden. Falcon was *Lord Rowan*? The Queen's Blade? When tensions between humans and fae were at their peak, he had killed dozens of mages. He'd been unstoppable, until the queen had put up his sword when she agreed to the treaty between our worlds. Even though there was peace when I was an apprentice, Matthew had told us ghoulish stories of the murders the Blade had committed—one more reason, for him, why the fae were too dangerous to coexist with humanity. I remembered the impassive figure in gold armor at the queen's back, mouth hard and unforgiving.

I'd thought he was some minor fae trapped outside the feygate. I'd been riding around with him for the last day and a half, devil-may-care. I'd let him walk me through a gate here, with no idea if it led where he said. I maybe needed to develop some trust issues, because the ones I had were clearly inadequate.

"And you are?" Lady Hawthorn was looking at me, head tilted questioningly. She had perhaps already asked once.

"Morgan Tenpenny." I hoped my voice was steady.

"Oh! How delighted I am to see you. You must come to Marcus at once. He will be so glad you found him, poor man. He was frantic to reach you. Follow me."

She turned, skirts trailing behind her, and started back up the staircase she had just swept down. Falcon—Lord

Rowan—and I followed. He looked at me inquiringly, and I shook my head. I wasn't certain what he was asking, and I didn't know what I was feeling—besides dismay and confusion. He had helped me, and that counted for something. What mattered was Marcus, and the Savannah flu, and Gwen and the girls. A nice comforting moment of succumbing to panic about fae assassins would have to wait until I had time, if I lived that long. If I didn't, well, it wouldn't be my problem.

The steps were marble, the railing some golden wood carved to resemble living vines, much like the bridge across the abyss outside. We went up two flights, and Lady Hawthorn led us down a hallway. She opened the last door on the right, and an unfortunately familiar smell assaulted me: antiseptic battling with sickness. It had been six years, but it took me right back to Dad with the hospice nurse sitting behind him, amber vials of medicine piled on the bedside table, his strong frame withered and small. Mom hunched over next to him, as if the cancer had shrunk her too, her fingers winding through his. I shook my head sharply.

"Did he bring the flu—the magic sickness here?" Falcon—*Rowan* turned to Lady Hawthorn.

"A magic sickness? My dear, such an imagination. People have been trying to make such a thing for centuries and no one's had any luck with it. Poor Marcus has a stomach cancer. We thought it was but dyspepsia for the longest time..." Her voice trailed off. I tried to shove away the memories of Dad's all-too-quick decline, and walked over to the bed.

"Marcus?" It was as bad as I remembered; another strong man I loved reduced to a frail shadow of himself. His gray hair had thinned since I'd seen him, and wrinkles etched deeper around his mouth and eyes. Smile lines were mixed now with lines carved by pain. His hands were spotted and thinner than I remembered.

His eyes opened and he rolled onto his side, bracing himself against the pillow behind him and reaching for the glass of water on the bedside table. He took a long swallow and then smiled a cut to my heart. "Morgan. You found me."

I shrugged. "I had help."

He looked over my shoulder and his eyes widened. The sclera were yellow. "Lord Rowan. It's been a long time."

Rowan nodded. "I regret the circumstances."

Marcus grimaced. "As do I." He looked over my shoulder at Lady Hawthorn, who turned gracefully to Rowan.

"Perhaps you would care for some refreshment, Lord Rowan?"

The former Queen's Blade shot me an unreadable look, then allowed himself to be led away.

I sat in the chair next to Marcus's bed and took his hand. His fingers were bony and as wasted as the rest of him. The plain gold band was missing from his ring finger, but a deep groove in the flesh marked where it had rested for decades, even after David died. A flash of gold chain at his neckline made me suspect it had just migrated. He searched my face, then released my hand to fumble a pill from one of the vials by his bedside. The pill had a faint silvery shine, perhaps cast to work faster.

"Marcus...I would have come sooner if I'd known you were..." I trailed off. I couldn't have come sooner. I hadn't known he was alive, much less where he was.

He swallowed the pill, grimacing at the taste, then followed it with a sip of water. "I didn't want you to know—any of you. I could spare you having to watch...this." His face relaxed as the medicine took effect. "I came here to die on my own terms." Perhaps that was so, but he'd vanished from my life after Matthew tried to start another fae-human war.

I swallowed my resentment. It was done, and nothing could change it. Even if I'd been here, there was nothing I could have done that he wasn't already doing. I wasn't a healer, and even healers couldn't heal cancer. "You didn't call me to...say goodbye?"

His smile was a wretched thing. "If things had worked out as I wished them, you would have gotten a letter and a few things after I died. Easier on both of us that way. No, I called you because of the girls." I looked at him, still trying to digest that he was dying, that he'd had no intention of letting me know until it was too late. Easier? Easier for him, maybe. "Your sister's girls," he clarified.

"What about them?" My hand went unthinkingly to my heart, where the tattoo that linked me to them lay quiescent. They were still safe, for now.

He tracked the movement and smiled faintly. "Have you already done something to protect them? Good. They'll need it." He drew in a deep breath, winced, and rested a hand on his abdomen. "Rose saw something about them."

"Who's Rose?"

"She's the caster that built this place."

"*One* caster built all this?"

He smiled. It was a feeble shadow of his old smile, but it was real, and some of the weight compressing my chest lifted. "Lady Hawthorn helped some, but yes—Rose did most of the work, back in the fifties." Damn. I had done a few things, magically, that I was proud of but I couldn't conceive of undertaking something this complex. I couldn't conceive of having the vision to even think of the possibility in the first place.

And she had done it decades ago, and kept it secret all the time since—just as much of an undertaking, really. "In the fifties? How old is she?"

"She died twenty years ago." He shifted uncomfortably while I tried to reconcile what he'd just told me. How had this woman known about the girls twenty or more years before they were born? "Rose told Damana—Lady Hawthorn—that they are at the heart of a storm that encompasses Faerie and earth, and they are the only way out."

"What, some kind of prophecy?"

"I suppose so." He closed his eyes and lay back against the pillow. "Where are they?"

"Underhill with their mother."

"You must get them out. If the queen becomes aware of their importance..." His eyes flicked open. "For that matter, you must not let the Association get their hands on them either. Some would want to use them as a weapon against Faerie. They don't deserve that."

"You always told me prophecy was bullshit."

He smiled, a ghost of his former grin. "That was before I met Rose."

"When did you meet her, exactly?" If she had died twenty years ago, around or slightly before I was his student, and he had told me then that there was no such thing as prophecy...I was confusing myself.

"When I first came here, after I left New York." He sighed. "She's not a ghost, precisely." Another thing he'd told me was bullshit. "She tied herself to Strangehold before she died, and she just...never left. I'm not entirely certain how she did it. And the thing about the girls—It's not exactly prophecy, it's that Rose isn't anchored in time the way the rest of are. Magic leaks from here into our world, but it's not a one way trip. Some of it comes back, and when it does, she gets images. Fragments of things that have happened, or will happen, or may happen..."

"Magic leaks from here into our world?"

"And into Faerie. You're at the source, Morgan. The source of all magic." He smiled again, and his face transformed. I remembered this expression from when he taught me; when he was making a point he was particularly excited about it, he lit up. "It's not just a theoretical plane. We're *here*."

"Amazing." No wonder the magic outside had been so strong. I sat back, awed. Whoever this Rose was, she had clearly been—was?—a caster of incredible vision.

He took another sip of water. His hand shook, and some of it slopped over the edge of the glass, but when I leaned forward to help him, he glared at me. "Get the girls out of there, and teach them everything you can. They'll need it. About Rowan—he's dangerous, Morgan. He's deadly. I've seen him kill. Why is he with you?"

"We're just traveling together until we can get underhill. I didn't know he was the Queen's Blade. Listen, Marcus, I can't just go into Faerie and grab the girls. The feygates are closed." I filled him in on everything that was happening outside of Strangehold—the Savannah flu, Eliza's sickness, Gwen's coming to me for help—Rowan trapped outside the feygates. Marcus's expression turned inward as I spoke until I had nothing left to tell him.

"Fuck!" He turned his head to the side and clenched his shaking hand. "And I can't do a damn thing to help."

I took his hand. "You have to take care of yourself, Marcus."

"It's not enough." He sighed. His eyelids fluttered down again and his chin sagged onto his chest. I let my fingers slide down to his wrist to feel the reassuring beat of blood in his veins, and then I stood as quietly as I could and left.

*

It took some wandering around before I found the kitchen. I was thirsty and I wanted some time to sit and come to terms with the fact that Marcus was dying and a dead Tolkien nerd thought my nieces were important to world events. I went down endless staircases, down long hallways, and more by luck than design, I stumbled across the smell of baking bread, and after that, I followed my nose.

A square of warm yellow light spilled out of a doorway at the end of a hall, along with the yeasty bread smell. Maybe there would be coffee if I was lucky. I made for the door, then stopped before I crossed the threshold. Low voices conferred—Rowan and Hawthorn. It was rude to listen in, but under the circumstances, I wasn't going to let that keep me from finding out more about either of them. Rowan had not deceived me about who he was—he had said I could call him Falcon, not that it was his name—but nor had he volunteered any additional information. Then again, I wouldn't be eager to tell anyone about my illustrious career as an assassin either, if I had one.

"...thinks you're dead."

"My dear young man, that is entirely by design. I am content to stay here with my Rose and leave all the rest of it behind. Politics are so tiresome. We have guests enough through Strangehold to keep me entertained, and I don't miss the court at all. *You* must know, if you have left your former post."

"The problem with a weapon that thinks is that it may come to think its wielder wrong."

"The one who wielded you was never one to let a weapon go easily."

"Nor did she this time."

"Well, you may stay here as long as you like, but your human friend may need some help. Marcus has bad news for her, I fear. Family, you know."

"I'm afraid I don't." His voice was icy.

"Oh, hrm, yes, well. Forgive me, I had forgotten the manner of your upbringing." I didn't believe that for a moment.

"Do not hold my blood against me, and I won't hold yours against you." For the first time he sounded like a killer. He spoke quietly, but his voice dripped menace.

She trilled a laugh that sounded genuinely amused. "I wouldn't dream of it, my dear. I am *hardly* in a position to cast stones. And in turn, I won't hold your attempt to threaten me in my home against you. Oh here, now, none of that. Stand up, you're forgiven. I said I wouldn't hold it against you." The fae took hospitality very seriously, and guest threatening host was a serious *faux pas*.

I decided this was an opportune time to take a few noisy steps down the hall and into the kitchen. Hawthorn's eyes were still sparkling with amusement, but they dimmed as she turned to me. "Are you well, my dear? He is *very* changed. It must be a shock to you."

The sympathy in her voice brought tears stinging to the corners of my eyes, when in front of Marcus himself they had remained dry. "How long does he have?" My voice was rougher than I liked.

"Rose does what she can for him, but what she can do is mostly keep him comfortable. He might have a few months yet." The grim set to her mouth said she didn't really think it would be that long.

"I appreciate what you both have done for him."

"He is a very old friend, and always welcome here, no matter how long the stay." Or how short, I filled in. "May I get you anything? Water? Wine?"

"Coffee would be welcome."

"Certainly." She walked to a counter and started fussing with a kettle and press, her silver ball gown incongruous with the domesticity of the task.

Rowan looked at me, his face impassive, but I sensed wariness in him—or at least none of the ease which we had previously enjoyed.

"Marcus tells me my nieces are in trouble, and I need to get to them." I had meant to work my way into it more subtly. Oops. "So if you still need to get underhill, looks like I'm headed that way myself."

A mirthless smile twisted his lips. "You don't fear traveling with the Queen's Blade?"

I shrugged as casually as I could. "You said you're done with it, and I believe you."

The smile relaxed into something a little more real. "Then I thank you."

"Well, as long as we're both—" I stopped and looked at him. The fae didn't thank *anyone*, and they didn't like it if you thanked them. It was a thing.

"I have lived overhill for some decades now," he said. "I have learned to be flexible."

"Coffee!" Hawthorn pushed down the plunger on the press and poured a stream of dark, bitter coffee into a delicate blue cup. "Would you care for some, Rowan?" He shook his head, and she passed me the cup and set the press next to me. "In ordinary times, I would send you straight to your sister and her children, but Rose tells me our little back door won't be useful to you at the moment."

"Is it closed like the feygates?"

Her smile was charmingly smug. "The queen would have to know about it to close it like that. Unfortunately, one of the ways we conceal our door is by moving it about—or Rose tells me Faerie moves around our door, actually, but the result is quite the same. As it stands now, the door would still get you underhill, but until it moves, you would be stuck in the queen's gaol. We had occasion once to retrieve someone from the oubliette, and I'm afraid it still resets there sometimes," she added, seeing Rowan's horrified expression.

"If you could direct it to the oubliette, couldn't you direct it to Gwen's home?"

Hawthorn shook her head regretfully. "Rose could do it when she was alive, but now I'm afraid she doesn't have the power for it."

"Could she use mine?"

Hawthorn's eyes narrowed speculatively, but then she shook her head. "She thinks she could do it, but you'd be exhausted afterward, and no use to your sister's children. Don't worry. We'll think of something." She paused again. "And we will do it quickly, because Rose says it must be soon."

*

Hawthorn gave me a room just down the hall from Marcus's, and Rowan one next to mine. There was a connecting door, about which I felt ambivalent, but it was locked, about which I felt just fine. I did believe Rowan was done with his former career, and I didn't think he wanted to hurt me, but—he had been the Queen's Blade. I had trouble reconciling one of the fae bogeymen with the person I'd come to know, albeit briefly. I'd heard horror stories about him, tales from the days when humans and fae were at each other's throats. He'd killed mages, he'd killed assassins sent to kill him; he *was* one of the fae excesses that Matthew had cited as reasons humans should break the treaty.

I'd thought Matthew was all talk and bluster, right up until the day he tried to drive a sidheblade into the heart of a fae lord, one of the queen's nephews. We'd been part of the Association's guard for the fae visitor, which had made it worse. I'd tried to stop him; Marcus had *actually* stopped him. Seeing Marcus again brought it all back.

That bare recital of the facts didn't cover how it had felt, though. Matthew, Eliza, and I had shared a terribly grotty two bedroom apartment within walking distance of the Association's building in New York. We'd work with Marcus in the day and stay up late discussing magical theory over take out. Eliza was always terrifyingly competent and Matthew was our innovator. He could see ways of casting that never occurred to me and put them together into something new. One night I had come home to the two of them giggling and toasting each other with mugs full of some wretched Bordeaux; they had come up with a spell to keep roaches out of the apartment. I had thought Matthew's reaction to the fae—I hadn't let myself really believe that it was hatred—was a close-minded phase that he would get over in time. I had been wrong.

The nephew had lived, or nothing any human could have done would have appeased her. The Council of the Association banished Matthew to an island off the coast of South Carolina as punishment for breaking the treaty, and that was that. The Association didn't fuck around with banishment; Matthew would die if he set foot on the mainland ever again. I'd tried, once, to get in touch. It hadn't worked.

His trial had been awful. Marcus had to testify. He'd loved us all, but Matthew was his especial pride and clearly who Marcus had seen as heir to his Council seat and perhaps one day as head of the Association: strong in his powers and brilliantly flexible with his application of magic. He'd been capable of the most delicate manipulation, tying strands of power into complicated knots far beyond anything I could accomplish. Matthew had been so clearly destined for greater things. It had broken Marcus to see his prize pupil banished, having betrayed his teachings, and he had released us all and stopped taking students.

Eliza and I had finished our studies with another caster from the Council, under a glum cloud of sorrow. We'd kept on living in our roach-free apartment, and we kept sharing a room because neither of us could bear to move into Matthew's space, but the rest of our time there was haunted by his absence. The third cog in our little triangular gear was gone, having betrayed the Association and us. I'd been shocked, and grieving—and afraid to admit I was grieving, because what he'd done was treason, even if it hadn't succeeded. And I was so angry at him, for what he'd done to me and Eliza, and to Marcus.

And now Marcus was dying. I had to tell Eliza, as head of the Association, and as my friend. If my cell phone didn't work in Strangehold, I'd just have to summon a mirror link. I dialed her number. To my pleased surprise, it started ringing. It kept ringing, so long that I expected voicemail to pick up, but it didn't. Finally, a male voice on the other end answered. "Hello?"

"May I speak to Eliza? This is Morgan Tenpenny."

"You—you can't speak to her." I recognized the voice now: Jakub Kaminski, Eliza's right hand man. His voice was rough with exhaustion, and broken, and my chest contracted even before he went on. "I'm sorry to have to tell you this over the phone, Morgan, but she's dead."

"Oh, no." I clenched nerveless fingers on the phone to keep it from sliding out of my hand. First Helen, then Marcus's illness, and now Eliza... "But I just talked to her yesterday."

"It hits fast. It's hit them all fast. Morgan...are you coming back any time soon?"

I hesitated, surprised and bereft, but then it occurred to me: Jake was in his twenties. Casters generally lived a long time. He had expected a few more decades at Eliza's side before he had to be in charge. Another thought—was there no one more senior to help him? Had they all died too? "How soon do you need me?"

"Now would be okay." He sniffed and I pictured red-rimmed eyes. The scope of it was too much for me to imagine, and I thought about how awful was that luxury, to not know just yet who had died, how many I had to mourn.

"I'm coming back," I said. "I'm—I'm on my way to get my nieces, do you understand? But as soon as they're safe, I promise, Jake, I'm coming back. You don't have to do this alone."

He took a long, hitching breath, and I thought I was not the only one trying not to cry. "Morgan, it's awful. Please come quick."

"I will. As soon as I can. I will."

He hung up without saying goodbye.

I had to save my nieces, and then I had to help whatever was left of the Association. Rose thought my nieces were the key to finding a way out of the storm. Would there be anyone left when the storm was past?

*

The library at Strangehold was a researcher's dream. There were stacks upon stacks of books in old leather bindings. The shelves were packed with books hardbound in cloth, books with glossy paper covers, and mimeographed pamphlets. Hawthorn had showed me tablets loaded with articles and books, and a computer—Strangehold didn't have internet access, but the entire catalog was sorted by topic, author, and location in the library, in addition to less useful-to-me categories, like color and font.

For all the resources available to me, I was no closer to an answer about how to get underhill than I had been three hours earlier, when I started running down references to gates, feygates, boosting other casters' spells, the faerie court, and, a little guiltily, because I didn't really have time and it wasn't relevant, the Queen's Blade. Not that I found much. There was a brief description of the position, which was pretty much what I'd thought it was, the queen's assassin and bully, excuse me, her champion of blood, and of the first to hold it, lord Ashtree. How he had left the position was not described, nor his successors; "others have followed, as the title is assigned at the queen's whim." Not much I hadn't known or guessed already.

I filled most of a legal pad with notes and speculations, but none of it would congeal into a solution. Anything I—or Rowan, though he hadn't offered—could do would drain us, and I wanted both of us at full battle readiness to get Gwen and the girls away. I closed my eyes in the hope that a solution would write itself across my itchy eyelids, preferably in letters of flame so I would be sure to pay attention. When it didn't, I stood up and stretched, spine popping, and gathered up my notes. I retraced my steps through Strangehold. Marcus might not be able to help magically, but he'd been a caster for longer than I'd been alive, and one of the best. He might have a suggestion, and in any case, it would do me good to talk it out.

Marcus was awake and sitting up when I came in. This time the smell of sickness didn't hit me quite so hard. A half-eaten bowl of soup sat on the bedside table, and he turned from the window at my knock. The view was only a courtyard full of potted plants, but warm yellow light that approximated the sun streamed in through the windows anyway.

He listened while I laid out the problem. "We don't have to use Strangehold's back door. It would just be convenient," I finished. "If we could break through a feygate—or if you know another way to get underhill—"

He shook his head slowly, eyes focused inward. "No, nothing comes to mind. If the queen has barred the way, no spell that you or I could throw together can breach it. Faerie is in part an extension of her will, and we can't directly contradict it. Rose's workaround is subtle in its randomness, and that might be our best bet." His attention came back into the room. "I'll think about it, Morgan. We'll come up with something. It's just a question of finding the right lever."

"If we could find a way to focus the magic, like using a lens to intensify light..."

"You may have something there. Send Hawthorn to me when you leave—she may have a suggestion I can bend to our purpose so you won't be completely wrung out when you get there."

I rose to leave, but he said, softly, "Have you heard anything else from outside?"

My damned eyes were stinging again, and despair pressed the air out of my chest, but I couldn't lie to him. "Yes. Marcus—Eliza's gone. She died last night. I don't know who else is dead."

He laced his thin fingers together and bent over his lap so all I saw was the top of his head. I slipped out of the door to leave him alone with his grief.

But my own wasn't far away. I needed a distraction. Luckily I had one—my tattoos needed to be replenished before we left Strangehold, whether to Faerie or back to Atlanta. I wasn't going to risk using the torrent of magic outside, but it was calmer inside the hold—filtered by Strangehold itself somehow. I went looking for Hawthorn. At least overhill, it wasn't polite to just barge into someone else's home and start using magic, and I needed to pass on Marcus's request.

I found her and Rowan in the kitchen—what was it about kitchens that made people gravitate toward them? Even the fae, even in a place as strange as this? They looked as though they'd been having a discussion, but

Hawthorn was happy to tell me the way to her spell room before she went to Marcus. Rowan offered to accompany me, I agreed, and we were off.

Strangehold had a perfect room for casting. So many spells required a circle to contain or intensify the energy. Like many casters, I had a permanent circle in my workroom—in my case it was a circle painted on the floor of my seldom-used guest room, under a throw rug I moved whenever I had a more complicated ritual to undertake.

My circle was mainly used to intensify magic since energy near my home was diffuse and I needed ritual to guide the forces. There were different traditions—followers of the Order of the Golden Dawn, wiccans who approached magic as part of their religion, among many others—but no matter what casters called themselves or what rituals they used, the aim was the same: to manipulate magical energy to change the world.

This circle far outshone my ring of paint on the guest room floorboards. It was inlaid into the floor in a mosaic of different colored stone. Empty brackets on the walls, ready for candles, marked the cardinal points—if this places could be said to have anything like East or West. A fountain burbled quietly in one corner. Water trickled down a flowering hawthorn tree carved in marble. Next to it, a raised platform built of golden wood housed a few chairs. An observer's station? But no one was there now.

"What do you need to do?" Rowan asked.

"Our magic overhill is slow. A lot of human casters prepare spells ahead of time so we'll have them if we need them." I remembered Helen's bracelet and pulled it out of my pocket to show him. "Helen put hers on a bracelet. A lot of people wear them as jewelry. I used to, too."

"But now you wear them on your skin. It seems unusual. Why?"

"Jewelry can be taken off you." A flash of memory: Matthew yanking the necklace off my neck, the burn of the chain against my skin. My frustration and helplessness as he knotted my wards in a flow of energy, cutting me off from my spells. I hadn't been able to stop him, and he almost started a war between Faerie and the Association.

I dismissed the past and pulled up my sleeve. Five stars arched across the inside of my right wrist. Rowan leaned in to take a closer look.

"You've woven strands of magic in the image itself."

"Yes. When I pull energy into the tattoos, it directs it in the configuration I need. Cast a glamour." He raised an eyebrow and summoned an image of stars and planets dancing in the air in front of us, as though a cartoon character had been conked on the head.

The central star on my wrist pulsed silver and vibrated gently against my skin.

"So you know when spells are worked around you." He nodded approvingly and banished the glamour of stars.

"Yes." I tugged my sleeve down. "There's a theory that keeping that much magic so close all the time could be harmful, and there is a chance a spell could backfire and hurt me, but I think it's worth the risk." I walked over to the observer's station and set Helen's bracelet by the fountain so her spells wouldn't clash with mine inside the circle. A pang of loss shot through me—this was all that was left of her. The quartz clinked against the stone hawthorn. Tiny stone roses bloomed as well, carved on the fountain amongst the hawthorn's flowers.

The center of the circle was marked with an inlaid sunburst pattern in different colored stones. I folded myself down into a crossed leg position and opened myself to the energy around us. Rowan dropped to the floor across from me.

"All I'm going to do now is pull energy into the pathways I set up when I had them inked." I closed my eyes and reached out. The energy here flowed plentifully and easily. The ouroboros over my left shoulder was nothing more than a well for magic, so I'd never be caught without a spell if there was no leyline nearby. I'd nearly drained it at Helen's house. The oak tree over my heart had once been just a well also, but now it was more. I started to direct energy there, and then Rowan joined his magic to mine.

Here in Strangehold, built at the source of magic, both of us were stronger. Our combined power sent me reeling internally. If Helen's power had been elegant loops and Matthew's intricate knots, Rowan's was a wave that washed over and through me. I felt like I was floating. It was euphoric—*I* was euphoric. The room spun. I felt so full of magic that the tattoos could crawl right off of me and my skin might split. What would emerge, better and more powerful? I sent energy to all my tattoos at once, and they tingled, full, but almost I thought I could send them *more*.

"Stop," I croaked, and managed to tear myself apart from our shared energy. It was hard to let go, and I felt deflated when I did, sagging back into my skin, into only myself. I opened my eyes and slumped back, chest heaving. I was sweating and—I looked down—my tattoos were *glowing*, the colors of the ink illuminated by silver light. That had never happened before. The oak tree on my chest shone through the fabric of my t-shirt. It had changed. Among the branches, two acorns hung between green leaves.

I looked up to see Rowan staring at the glowing ink outline of the tree through my shirt. He was a picture drawn in silver for a moment, and then the light began to fade, lingering in his eyes.

"Forgive me," he said. "I didn't expect...that."

"I didn't think we'd be able to work together at all," I said, sidestepping what had just happened. Had it felt the same to him? "It surprised me when you could help with the wards around Helen's house. My understanding was the fae and human approach to magic is too different to blend, even if the energy we use is the same."

"Were I only fae, that might be the case." He watched me closely.

"You had a human parent? Like the girls?"

"Only it was my mother who was fae, and my father a mortal man."

"How is it that you..." I tried to think of a tactful way to ask it, but gave up. "Then how were you the Queen's Blade?"

He turned his hands over. The fading silver light picked out scars over his knuckles. "I don't claim to know the workings of her majesty's mind, but...I think she saw it as an honor she gave me." He sighed. "And at the same time it spared any other from the task."

Pity lanced me. Even so, I was aware that I was pitying someone who had killed a lot of people. "How did you quit? I always thought it was because of the peace with humans, but it wasn't, was it?"

He looked at me and smiled, but shook his head. He stood, and offered me a hand. "You are replenished, are you not? We should find Hawthorn. I believe I hear the dinner bell."

I heard nothing, but I took his hand and let him pull me up, my legs stinging from sitting for so long on the stone floor. He could keep his secrets until he wanted to tell me.

And now, I was ready, if only we could find a way to act.

*

I woke up all at once, unsure what time it was. Strangehold's light was all artificial, of course, but the windows mimicked sunlight, and by that metric it was shortly before dawn. I wasn't sure why I had awakened; I vaguely remembered a dream where a woman I didn't know but immediately liked had been telling me something urgent, but it slipped further away the harder I tried to hold on to it.

Someone knocked, then shoved the door open before I had a chance to say a word, or do more than pull the blanket up reflexively. Lady Hawthorn swept in, almost as elegant as ever in a long nightdress and robe; but strands of hair poked out of her disheveled braid and her eyes were wide. "Morgan! You must come at once. Dress and arm yourself. The way is open." She took my arm and leaned closer. "Your nieces! The time is now. Hurry!"

I leapt out of bed. Her urgency cleared the befuddlement of sleep, and I pulled on jeans and my boots as she waited, all but tapping her foot, then retreated to the bathroom to change into a sports bra and shirt, and shove my hair into a ponytail. My tool bag was next to the bed, and I slung it over my shoulder. The sidheblade waited in my bracelet, and my tattoos were fully charged. I was as ready as I could be.

Hawthorn led me into the hall, where Rowan was waiting for us. He was dressed not for earth, but for Faerie; he wore the archaic clothes of the fae court—doublet, breeches, knee-high boots, all in dark gray—and was armed with a sword and a dagger. That I could see, that is; doubtless he had other weapons concealed somewhere on his person. A leather satchel dangled off one shoulder and he crammed the other arm through the loose strap as we half-walked half-ran.

"He never should have done it—oh, the idiot man!—but he has and we must make the most of it or it is all for naught. Rose says he can't hold it for long, and the door may well reset as soon as he lets go." She caught up her skirts to move faster and I followed behind her.

"Hawthorn—what has he done? Who?" Although I had a sinking presentiment that I knew.

"Marcus has provided Rose the energy she needs to secure the door underhill, the idiot, and he has almost certainly killed himself as well."

"Can she return the energy?" My breath caught in my throat. *Oh, Marcus...*I was pretty sure already that she couldn't, but I knew jack shit about ghosts, really, so maybe there was a possibility...

"No. He has pulled it straight from the source outside our walls." Hawthorn's long braid lashed from side to side as she shook her head. Her eyes shone with tears, but none fell. "If she could save him, she would, but now we can only make sure that his actions are not wasted. Here." She pressed a flat glass disc into my hand. "The door back is different from the door there; it moves at entirely random intervals. This will help you find it, once you have your family." I shoved the disc into my pocket.

She flung open the double doors to the workroom, and Rowan and I followed behind her. It was a familiar scene from my youth recast as a nightmare: Marcus in a fully-drawn circle, complete with incense and candles, and runes of power lit in silvery light so bright I didn't even need to summon my caster's vision to see them. The whites of his eyes were tinged red from burst capillaries and blood dripped from his nostrils. As sick as he was, the effort was too much for him. The silvery light blurred and I pushed tears from my eyes with the heel of my hand. If we couldn't stop him then I could at least try not to squander his sacrifice.

He looked right at me and nodded once. He was too far into the spell to speak. I wanted to tell him we would have found another way. I didn't know if it was true.

A door in the wall glowed bright silver. Rowan took my hand. I never would have thought to find comfort in the touch of the Queen's Blade, but I did. I squeezed his hand back.

Now. I twitched. The thought was not my own.

"She says go now!" Hawthorn yelled.

I wrenched the silver door open and took one last look at Marcus. He met my gaze and smiled, teeth stained red from the blood leaking from his gums. I turned forward, and Rowan and I crossed the threshold of the door into Faerie.

*

It was dark, wherever we were, and the thought crossed my mind that it would be a damn shame if after all that the door was still in the dungeons.

Rowan's hand tightened on mine. He might be having the same thoughts, or it might be the curse's hold on him returning after its absence in Strangehold. It must not be night in Faerie, because he hadn't become a falcon.

There was light behind us, so I turned. The faint silvery outline of a door glowed for a few seconds longer, fading away into nothingness. The light had illuminated the space we were in; a closet, big enough that I was fleetingly jealous for the storage—my house overhill had been built in the fifties, and the closets weren't spacious—with a few cloaks or robes hanging in one corner. I brushed the wooden walls with my free hand until I felt the door.

"Should we open it?" I whispered.

Rowan cocked his head, listening, and nodded. I dropped his hand, my palm suddenly cool without his warmth, and slowly pushed the door open. The hinges didn't creak, and the silence outside had a still, empty quality—no breathing, no slight movements. The room was opulent but the air was musty, and a thin layer of dust coated the furniture. Light spilled through slatted wooden blinds at the windows, but none of the lamps were lit.

Rowan followed me, looked around, and flinched, ever so slightly. "We're safe. No one will be here," he muttered.

"Do you know where we are?"

He ran one finger through the dust covering a chair. "These were my old rooms, when I was in the queen's favor. I had thought she would have gotten rid of them, or given them to someone else. How sentimental of her." His tone was dry, but a note of pain ran under it. But I doubted he would want to see pity from me.

"How close are we to Gwen's rooms?"

"If the court has not much changed since last I was here, we are but perhaps a ten minutes walk." He looked at my jeans, t-shirt, and backpack and frowned. I did look out of place next to him, but I hadn't had time to dress differently even if it had occurred to me.

He turned back to the closet we'd just emerged from and pulled out a coat. It was a dark brown duster with a high collar and panels of embroidered flowering branches running down it—rowan leaves, of course. I dropped my backpack and pulled it over my clothes, and he nodded. "Keep your head down and follow behind me. Hold your bag as though you are carrying something for me. If we encounter anyone, don't speak. I have not been to court in some years, but I was never forbidden it, so no one is likely to question us."

"All right." I took a deep breath and followed him to the door. He rolled his shoulders back and stood straight; I could almost see the role of Lord Rowan settling over him. He opened the door.

Graceful marble arches formed an open-air courtyard, and vines tipped with bright red blossoms twined around them, meeting in a lattice overhead. They were no plant I knew, but the fragrance was wonderful, something between honeysuckle and jasmine. Potted flowers in marble urns brightened the base of each column, and thick stands of lavender lined the walkways. Birds flitted from plant to plant, calling to each other, and bees buzzed a counter-point.

The court of Faerie wasn't the single palatial building I had envisioned, but a series of smaller structures that made a harmonious whole. The central building was the largest, and it must be where actual court was held, but the rest was a honeycomb of gardens and residences. Rowan's house was one of many, none of them so close that one would feel the press of one's neighbors, but none so far that one could entirely avoid them, either. Rowan looked around, then strode off through an arch down one of the paths. I followed, head down, but eyes darting from side to side. Every step brought a new beauty out of the corner of my vision, and I wished I could just sit and take it in and enjoy it. I thought of our last meal overhill before we went to Strangehold; the dim bar redolent with the stink of old beer, pop music playing faintly, too bland to be worth listening to, and soggy fries under electric light, and wondered how he had left this for that.

He walked purposefully, and while we passed a few other people, none of them did more than murmur a greeting and keep walking. They seemed wary; shoulders set, overly stiff and formal. It reminded me again of the bar, the wait staff looking at us suspiciously. The queen had shut the gates because of some threat. Had these people been attacked somehow? I kept my eyes downcast, though I itched to know who we passed, and whether they were a danger to us. The hair on the back of my neck and my arms wanted to stand straight up. What if someone called us out? Would they know I was here for Gwen and the girls? Every time someone walked by, my nerves ratcheted a bit tighter, until I half wanted to yell myself, just to break the tranquil stillness. We turned down another open path—how did the residents keep them all straight?—and Rowan's step sped up. I hoped that meant we were nearly there.

"Lord Rowan!" This greeting was not murmured but called out across the courtyard. Rowan stopped. The line of his back was stiff, but his voice was perfectly friendly when he answered.

"Lady Briar, I had no expectation of seeing you here." He bowed low, and she returned the courtesy. She was tall and lovely, with golden skin, hair the red of rose hips in the fall, and eyes the amber of a cat's. A certain tension in the set of her shoulders suggested she might be nervous.

"Nor I you. But I hope the pleasure is not lessened for being unexpected." She hesitated, glancing around. There was no one near but us, and me she ignored entirely. "You found it, then," she said softly.

This was the Briar who had told him about Strangehold. I kept my eyes on the flagstones beneath my feet, but sweat prickled along my upper lip. Would she try to stop us? To find out why he had needed to know about Strangehold? Then I sneered at my paranoia; of course she'd think he'd needed to get back to Faerie. He was here; that was explanation enough.

"You were most helpful, and I will not forget it. If you will excuse me—"

"If there is else you need, you have only to ask."

"If there is, I will."

"I want to help you."

"Delphine, I beg of you..."

She sighed. "Your mother was asking after you."

"Please give her my regards when next you see her." His voice was still perfectly polite, but suddenly infinitely colder. Lady Briar must have heard it as well, because she begged her leave.

I felt her eyes on my back as she returned the way she had come. Rowan muttered something under his breath and started walking again. I no longer cared for the beauty of the garden, only for finding our goal. Not long after we came to a residence much like all the other residences we had passed. I didn't see anything marking it as an ambassador's home, or the embassy of overhill. I ached that I didn't even recognize Gwen's house. I'd been reluctant to come here first because of my connection with Matthew, and then when Gwen married Elm, I hadn't wanted to scuttle her chances of finding acceptance from her husband's family. From here, it seemed so shortsighted. So stupid. This was her life, and I hadn't been a part of it. I'd apologize when I saw her, and I wouldn't be such an idiot in the future. I touched the oak tree over my heart for reassurance, and promised myself.

Rowan did something—what, I wasn't exactly sure, but the warm feel of his magic buzzed against my nerves, an echo through all my ink of the power we'd shared in Strangehold. The star over the pulse of my wrist vibrated softly. A moment later, the door opened to reveal a handsome man: long blond hair, luridly blue eyes, high cheekbones, lean and tall—my brother-in-law. Elm. His eyes widened as he took in his visitor, and his face paled. I don't think he even saw me. "Lord Rowan! I—what brings this honor?"

"May we come in?"

Elm looked past Rowan at that *we* and noticed me. His eyebrows climbed up his forehead. "Well. Yes, by all means, come in. You are welcome here." He was looking at Rowan as he spoke, but the last was said to me. It was a neat trick, and I'm not sure how he managed it.

He stood aside to let us enter, and as I walked closer, I saw his eyes were rimmed with red. I touched the tattoo over my chest without meaning to; the girls were still well. But I had no such assurances as to my sister. He shut the door firmly behind us and locked it.

"Guinevere told me you swore to protect them," he said abruptly.

"I did, and I mean to keep my word." There was no immediate need to tell him that a dead woman had told us they were key to the future of Faerie. There would be time for that later.

His face relaxed, but then his brows drew together as he looked at Rowan. "And you, have you taken up the mantle you cast aside? Did she send you for my daughters?"

"I am here as a favor to Morgan," Rowan said, not altogether gently. "I am no longer the queen's to send. Have you reason to suspect she wishes your children ill?"

"Gwen thought so. I thought her fears were foolish, but now..." His lids slid closed over blue irises, and tears spiked his eyelashes but didn't spill. "I don't know what to think. Morgan—you may not see your sister again."

I sucked in a breath, a wordless protest against the sudden hole in my chest. I couldn't accept it—another loss, the worst loss. It wasn't that I thought she was immune to harm, but on a cellular level, I didn't believe in a world where she didn't exist. I struggled to get a handle on myself. He had said *may* not see her. I managed to force words through the wall of my disbelief. "What happened?"

The beautiful blue eyes opened, still gleaming with grief. "The queen's creatures took her."

Next to me, Rowan went very still.

"How is that possible? She's done nothing wrong. She's the ambassador. She should have been safe." Gwen was the representative of the Association. They were not the only group of casters treating with the fae, nor were they necessarily the most powerful. But they were the biggest official organization of casters in North America, and Gloriana could not possibly think to disappear her without experiencing repercussions. But she had shut the feygates; maybe she meant to close off Faerie and earth forever and didn't care what the Association or any other group would say about it.

"What about other ambassadors from overhill?" I looked to Elm. "Is she the only one taken?"

"Some of the others were brought to the queen, but Guinevere was the only one she kept." Lord Elm's shoulders heaved, and then he stood very still. He looked at Rowan. "You know better than I what will happen to her."

Rowan took my hand. "I will do my best to find her. It may be that we can yet retrieve her." *Kept* did not mean *dead*. Not yet.

"I have protested formally," Elm said. "For whatever good that will do. But my expectations are not high." He walked to a closet on the far end of the room and pulled out two camping-style backpacks. "Take the girls away from here, before her eye falls on them too."

"You could come with us," I said.

"No." He wiped his face. "I mean to disguise their absence for as long as I may. No one will look for them if they do not seem to be missing. Besides, from here I can better aid their mother, if there is aid to be found."

I took his hand and tried to imbue the simple clasp of hands with the gratitude I felt to him at that moment. It was only one chord of a symphony of worry, grief, and hope, but he was doing what he could for his family. I had been so focused on all the reasons the match was a bad idea, I had never stopped to think about why Gwen loved him. I understood a little better now.

His fingers tightened around mine, and then he extricated himself. "Come with me. Their rooms are here."

We followed him deeper into the residence. Here and there I could see touches of Gwen: in the gathered irises in a vase—her favorite flower, in the battered paperbacks on a bottom shelf, below shelves of gleaming leather books and small vases and miniature works of art. A narrow hall led to bedrooms; one I assumed to be Gwen and Elm's, as he pushed open the door of the other. Two girls clad in tunics and trousers were sprawled across twin beds in a scene that would have fit in anywhere overhill except they held a book and a metal locking puzzle instead of cell phones. They sat up as we walked in and looked questioningly at their father.

For a moment I wanted to protest that he had the wrong room—these girls were far too old to be my nieces. But time ran differently in Faerie, and these were the girls. Two pairs of solemn eyes stared out at me, one a brilliant green, and one as brown as my own. I had thought I would have more time to know them as they grew. I wasn't good at guessing children's ages—they varied so much as individuals, you could put a five and seven year old together and not be sure who was older—but if I had to try to pin them down, they looked to be around ten.

Igraine's bright green eyes shone against olive skin and dark hair like mine. People were going to think she wore contacts her entire life. Iliesa had Elm's high cheekbones and pointed ears, and blonde hair the exact shade of my mother's. I cleared my throat against the sudden lump in it.

"I'm your aunt Morgan," I told them. "You were babies the last time I saw you."

"They are aging quickly even for Faerie," their father murmured. "Guinevere and I speculated why, but..." He spread his hands.

"We remember you." Igraine's green eyes were solemn.

"You were so young." I swallowed. "I'm glad. I'm looking forward to knowing you better."

"You will be staying with your aunt for a time." Lord Elm tried to force a smile for his daughters.

"Why? Where's Mom?"

"She has had to go away, and I'm not sure when she will be coming back." He knelt and embraced them both. "No matter what happens, always remember that your mother and I love you very much."

Now they looked frightened—and how could they not, after a statement like that? Igraine opened her mouth to ask a question, but a melodious chime rang in the front hall. Lord Elm was on his feet in an instant, his face drawn. "All of you," he murmured, "stay very quiet. Please, make no sound."

His footsteps echoed down the hall. I knelt down between their beds, and tried to look reassuring. They looked at me, then at each other, and some voiceless communication passed between them. Igraine reached over and took my hand. Rowan padded silently over to the door and motioned me over with a jerk of his chin. I squeezed Igraine's hand and joined him. He flicked his fingers and the star at my wrist tingled. I raised an eyebrow and he mimed shutting the door. A glamour, then, so the door would look closed from the outside.

We peered around the real door, my hand poised to close it. Lord Elm's back was to us. His head was bent over a piece of folded paper, and a person waited in the doorway. He had a crane's long neck and a bright spray of red feathers on the crown of his head, but from the shoulders down he was humanoid, except for the graceful wings folded at his back. They did not look big enough for flight, but this was Faerie, so I wouldn't have taken a bet. He was wearing what appeared to be livery in shades of green and gold.

"Of course I will come at once," Elm said, "but her majesty must excuse my daughters. They are unwell, and resting. The stress of their mother's absence has been very difficult for them." A slight movement pressed against my back. The girls had come to listen. I couldn't blame them, but I pressed a hand gently against Iliesa's shoulder when she would have crowded into the doorway with Rowan and me.

"Her majesty asked for all of you." The crane's voice was polite, but managed to convey disapproval regardless.

"They are *children*," Elm said, "and they are unwell."

The crane cocked his head. "Perhaps if I might look in on them..."

Elm straightened. "You doubt my word?"

"No! No, my lord, of course not. But in these difficult times, the queen requires all assurances."

"I must protest," Elm said, "in the strongest terms, this implication of dishonor. I have already brought the matter of the baseless imprisonment of my wife to the head of my House, and I assure you I will not hesitate to add this to my charge. The court will know how her majesty's servants impugn a lord of Faerie."

The crane's head ducked in a sinuous bow. "Nevertheless..."

Elm turned, back straight, and marched down the hall toward us. I grabbed Rowan's arm without thinking about it. He crooked his arm tighter so both of us were in front of the girls and the fingers on his free hand twitched. The glamour was still up, for whatever good that would do us. Would the crane be able to feel it? I looked over my shoulder; the girls were both all big eyes, but Igraine had something gleaming in her hand, and Iliesa held a wooden cane like a baseball bat. I held out a hand, silently urging them to wait.

Elm walked down the hall and didn't let even a momentary glance fall on the door we hid behind. His face was frozen in glacial offense. He opened the door I had assumed to be to his and Gwen's room and my teeth sank into my lower lip in an effort to keep from making a sound. Rowan looked down at me for an instant, his face grim.

Replicas of the girls lay on beds identical to the ones in this room. They were glamour, of course, but Elm had imbued them with enough of himself that they looked natural in sleep, shifting and breathing as if alive.

"Please don't wake them," Elm said. "They've been feverish. This is the first time they've been able to sleep."

Crane bowed. "Very well. They may rest. But we must not keep her majesty waiting any longer than we already have."

Elm bowed and strode off, not betraying his daughters' actual location with so much as a glance. Crane followed, long neck undulating with each step. How long had Elm been prepared for this? We listened as their footsteps dopplered away, as the door closed.

"Dad..." one of the girls whispered behind me.

"There's no time to lose," Rowan said. "We must go at once."

"But Dad—" Iliesa said.

"I'm sorry," I said to her, then turned to take in Igraine as well. "Your mother asked me to protect you, and your father asked me again today. It's not safe here for you, not right now. Until your parents are sure it's all right, you need to stay with me."

"We don't know you," Igraine said. Her voice was calm, but her fists were clenched at her sides. "I want Mom and Dad."

"And they want you too," I said. "But more than that, they want to be sure you're okay, and I can't guarantee that here. Please."

"If we wait here until another lackey comes back, you will find yourself suffering the queen's hospitality," Rowan said. "I have guested in her dungeon before, and you would not like it there—and if your mother is there, it will grieve her to see you."

"Igraine," Iliesa said quietly, and they traded another look that held a conversation. Igraine nodded, and relief blossomed in my heart. I'd have dragged them away if I had to, but that wasn't how I wanted to start their time with me, however long it ended up lasting.

"Do you have coats or cloaks? Preferably with hoods?" Rowan glanced toward a standing wardrobe in the corner of the room, and under his frown, they scrambled to find cloaks, in matching green with elm leaves in a paler shade all around the hem. "Pull the hoods forward to shadow your faces," Rowan instructed as he knelt to sever the embroidered hems. Iliesa flinched as the knife severed the fabric, but she hushed at a look from her sister.

"Come on," I said, once they were more-or-less disguised. We walked down the hallway, past the sleeping simulacra lord Elm had made. Iliesa shivered as she took them in. I picked up the packs their father had left for them and handed each girl one. Then I pulled the disc Hawthorn had given me from my pocket. I had hardly looked at it when she gave it to me. The disc fit comfortably in the palm of my hand, dichroic glass in shades of green, purple, and blue.

"How does it work?" Rowan asked.

I suppressed the urge to tell him he knew as much as I did, and sent a tendril of magic from the ouroboros knot at my shoulder into the disc. A tiny yellow light swirled out of the design and wandered to the left end of the disc, where it sat, pulsing gently. "Like a compass, I think. Let's follow it."

"You think?" Igraine's voice pitched high.

"We need to stay quiet and stick together," Rowan said. "I'll lead, with you girls behind me. Morgan, follow behind them. If we run across anyone, let me do the talking." I passed him the disc. He watched the light for a moment, then sighed and said in low tones, just to me. "I suppose we could not hope for the door to still be in my quarters. This way leads to the wild woods."

"Isn't that better than the dungeons, or behind the

queen's throne?"

He made a tiny gesture with one hand that I figured was the fae equivalent of warding off the evil eye. "Let us hope so." He started walking and the girls fell in behind him. They leaned toward each other, and one—I couldn't tell who, cloaked as they were—reached out and met the other's hand, reaching out toward her. My chest ached with worry for Gwen, for them, even for Elm, whom I hadn't thought enough of until now, and with the sense of impending grief to add to that which I already bore. I promised myself a chance to let loose and feel it—when the girls were safe away from Faerie. I started walking, the sidheblade bracelet a comforting weight at my wrist.

Rowan walked through the maze of archways and houses. A few fae watched from afar—lords and ladies in jewel-bright clothes, small winged creatures like a child's idea of a fairy, melds of people and animals, melds of people and trees, stranger things that were hard to describe. I kept my head down to keep myself from staring.

Rowan turned down a path that was gravel instead of flagstones. A flag of black fabric swathed a post at a crossroads and Rowan frowned at it for a long moment before shaking his head and walking on. We were moving away from the residences now. There were still a few outbuildings, and what looked like stables, and beyond that, fields. Roads led away, and a little town or village dotted a hill in the distance. But we were going the other way, toward the wood that smudged the horizon, blurring it with greens and blues.

The gravel path became a dirt trail, and the growth

around us got higher and wilder. The air smelled of grass and honey, and bugs buzzed in the plants. I felt eyes on the back of my neck, but no matter how I looked, I didn't see anyone. I drew closer to the girls. After perhaps half an hour of walking, the woods getting larger and clearer as we drew closer, Rowan stopped and turned back to all of us. His eyebrows were drawn together, a small line marring his smooth brow. "We must be careful from here on out," he said. "Stay close together and stay alert. This is the oldest part of Faerie, and there are things here outside even the queen's knowledge. And...something feels—off."

"Off?" I looked at him.

He shook his head. "It's been so long since I've been here, I'm not sure...Well. We need to be careful regardless. The woods do not reward carelessness kindly." He handed me the disc. "I don't know quite where the door will be. The wild wood changes and shifts. If anything happens, get the girls to the door."

"What about you?"

He lips twisted in a crooked not-quite-smile. "I'm safer underhill than any of you, at the moment. I'll find you when I can."

An awkward feeling of something not quite obligation twisted my chest. "Rowan—if it's easier—you don't have to find us. If you need to take care of things here—I know you were trying to get back here before we met—" I took a breath. "You've done so much to help us. To help me. Don't feel like you have to keep doing it."

His smile transformed into something real, something directed at me. I would almost have thought it glamour, but the star on my wrist was quiet. "Morgan," he said. "I have helped you because I want to. And I'll find you because I want to." The awkward feeling bloomed into something warmer. He turned back to the trail ahead before I could come up with a response. It didn't matter. I was glad he was with us.

"All right then. Let's find our door." I started walking. Igraine and Iliesa moved close behind me, and Rowan took tail this time.

"Mother told us about overhill," Igraine said softly as we walked.

"What did she say?" I prompted when she fell silent.

"She told us about movies," Iliesa said wistfully. "Like glamour tableaux, but the same every time."

"She told us about pizza," Igraine said.

"And French fries."

"Did she ever say anything about school?" I asked.

"We had tutors," Iliesa offered.

"We'll get all that sorted when we get home," I told them, but I wondered—did she tell them about me? Did she tell them about our parents? The thought of going home tensed the muscles in my shoulders; what was happening there? Who else had died? Time ran differently in Faerie. I selfishly hoped that by the time we got back overhill, maybe the Savannah flu would be dealt with, and I could take the girls home and just worry about them and their parents.

The trees drew closer around the trail. The shadows were blues and purples cast by a thousand shades of green, and the breeze was cool and smelled of pine. Some trees I recognized, but some had no counterpart on earth. I walked slowly, aware of every sound: birdsong, the rustle of leaves in the wind, the occasional louder crash of some small animal moving through the undergrowth, the distant gurgle of running water.

The trail seemed to be headed the same direction the glass wanted us to go, for now; I commented on it, and Rowan said, "If we are lucky, the woods are molding themselves to our intent. Sometimes the trail takes you where you want to go."

"What happens when it doesn't?" Igraine asked.

Rowan said nothing.

The splash of water rushing over rocks grew louder to our right, and the trail curved to meet it. The light on the disc agreed with the way we were heading, and I thought it was getting brighter. I stopped and held it up to show Rowan and the girls. Rowan's face lightened, and Iliesa said, "Does that mean we're near? Maybe we'll get through the woods and nothing will happen."

I bit my lip and reminded myself she'd never seen a horror movie. "We're not through yet," was all I said.

The trail bent around a stand of trees and the sight of the river stopped me in my tracks. It was not water lapping the pebbled banks, but blood. It was a disconcerting sight. My first, prosaic thought, besides *ewwww,* was *Why does it not clot?* "Where does it come from?" I asked instead.

"We are now at the beating heart of Faerie," Rowan said, right by my ear. I hadn't heard him walk up over the sound of the river. "The court is its face, the veneer of civilization over the primal instincts. Here, there is no such mask. We must be very careful."

The girls came closer, and we all stood for a moment and contemplated the awful expanse of liquid before us. Little insects, red and shiny as jewels, buzzed over the river, dipping down to skim the surface. The air had a metallic tang that coated the back of my mouth. *For forty days and forty nights/ He wade thro red blude to the knee,/ And he saw neither sun nor moon, / But heard the roaring of the sea,* I thought. The river wasn't so wide as in the Child ballad, though. I could see the opposite bank, where the trail resumed winding through the forest. But it was wide enough that there was a small island in the middle of the river. There was no obvious means across.

The light on the disc was pointing to the island rather than the trail on the other side.

It was too far to swing across the water, not that I saw convenient hanging vines in any case. A little boat failed to be serendipitously moored by the side of the trail, either.

"How do we cross?" Iliesa asked, and I blessed her for saying it so I didn't have to.

Rowan looked at the flowing blood for a moment longer, maybe hoping as I was for a bridge to suddenly rise from the river. He picked up a fallen branch and probed the liquid. "We wade across," he decided.

"Wade?" Iliesa's dismay was obvious, and I didn't feel much better about it.

"Ugh," said Igraine.

"Is it safe?" I met his gaze. His brow was furrowed again.

"As much as anything here. The river itself is only

blood and cannot harm you. I worry about what might live in it." He reached forward with the branch again, feeling for hazards. "Follow in my footsteps exactly."

He stepped into the river, blood splashing his boots. Igraine and Iliesa traded a look, then stepped in together, holding hands. I followed immediately, sidheblade at the ready in its silver bracelet. I wouldn't use it unless I must, because any fae with the slightest sensitivity could feel it, but if it came down to the girls' lives, I'd use it without hesitation, and let them find us.

The river squelched around my hiking boots, bloody mud sucking at my feet. Little stones or clumps of mud—or little blood fishes, for all I knew—hit against my ankles, not hard enough to knock me off balance, just enough to keep me worried they might. As we waded deeper, it sloshed over my boots, wetting my jeans and trickling down into my socks. It was horribly warm: body temperature. The girls shuddered in front of me, grasping at each others' hands as we lurched across the river. I wished I had someone's hand to hold. Instead I stumbled on, half my attention on the twins, half on the river, ready for something horrible and many-toothed to erupt from the liquid.

We were almost across with no worse than the fishes nipping at our ankles and the blood itself clotting against our skin. There wasn't a path out of the water—that would have been too easy—but roots looped in and out of the eyot's bank, forming handholds and footholds that were almost a ladder. Rowan could scramble up first, and then I could boost the girls and he could pull them up—

Blood eddied in front of us. Rowan tensed and flung a

hand out in warning. The girls froze, and I closed the short distance between us. Something rose from the river, head bent, black-furred shoulders rippling with muscle. Red streamed from it, slicking the fur back. Its head slowly raised, yellow eyes blinking away blood. I had expected a phouka or a jenny-in-the-water, but this was a great black dog with a heavy muzzle and fangs the length of my fingers at least. It loomed over us, taller than Rowan by half, and it was the black of a starless night, of the death of hope. It opened its jaws and a red tongue flopped out.

"Son of Faerie, you've strayed far from home," it rumbled. "Your choice of companions would interest your mother."

"She is not here, yath hound," Rowan called up at it, "and my companions are of no interest to anyone but me." I cupped the disc in the palm of my hand, looking at the island jutting out of the river, a tangle of trees and brush—as hard as it was to look at anything but the dog.

The yath hound laughed like the creaking of cemetery gates. "No princeling was ever so innocent." The glass glowed gently, the yellow light bright in front of us. The largest tree on the eyot was a great oak, its branches trailing vines and moss. The trunk was fat, so big around that all four of our group could have stood around it and maybe, if we stretched out our arms, our fingertips would brush. Lightning had struck it at some point, and the trunk had split. It was hard to see from this angle, but as I watched, faint yellow light washed over the crevice in the wood. There was our door.

"I'm no prince," Rowan snapped, "only a bastard

changeling, of no use to anyone except as a blade."

The hound yawned, showing its great teeth, sending a wave of charnel-house breath over us. "You cannot truly believe that, or you would not be here, attempting to move pieces about the game board. Other players will notice your move, son of Faerie. You will no longer be able to hide overhill." If we could get past the dog and pull ourselves up the bank, it would only take an instant to get to the tree.

"I was not hiding—" Rowan started, then stopped. For a long moment, the only sound was blood lapping against the bank, the buzz of insects, and the loud panting of the hound's breath. Rowan stepped closer to the great dog and tilted his head up at it. "On whose behalf are you here?"

"I could tell you it was my own, or that of Faerie itself, but I think you know better. Nothing happens here that your mother doesn't know of it, sooner or later, and for you, she would have it be sooner." I rolled my shoulders backward as surreptitiously as I could, and sunk my awareness into the sigils tattooed on my body. There was a band around my right bicep, a stylized, abstracted chain. I silently asked it to wake.

"I had not thought you leashed, by my mother or anyone else."

The yath hound laughed again, and the girls winced back against me. I put my hands on their shoulders, steadying them. "We all wear leashes, princeling. You can accept it, or fight against it, but in the end, you will be put to heel. Even your chess pieces here wear leashes." Its yellow gaze flicked to me and the girls. I would rather it had kept ignoring us. "Love, or vows, or vengeance—we are all bound."

"A pretty sentiment, but I gave up my bonds long ago."

The massive shoulders heaved as the hound shrugged. "If we all did as you, there would be anarchy."

Rowan stepped closer. "You're in my way."

"What seek you in this backwater piece of the woods?" The dog's eyes narrowed.

"Only to walk through it." Rowan held out his empty hands. The girls' shoulders trembled with tension.

"May we pass?" I said. Sometimes you really did just have to ask. I didn't expect it to be that easy this time, but we wouldn't know unless we tried.

The hound lowered its great head and its nostrils spread wide as it snuffled, breathing in my scent, and the girls'. "How interesting," it growled. "Everyone thinks these children sleep in their father's house, and yet here they are with you. And what *are* you?" Its yellow eyes widened and it leaned forward. I tensed.

"Just a visitor who wants to go home." The chain was ready.

It shook its great head, slaver flecking its red mouth. "My queen has shut the gates, so you cannot leave. Don't worry. You will find my queen's hospitality most thorough."

Right. That was enough of that. "I'm afraid not, hound." I flung my hand out and the chain spell solidified into a solid bar of energy. I pushed the hound back, blood splashing around its huge paws as it sank into the river mud. It roared in fury.

"Go!" I told Rowan. "Get the girls up there. I'll hold it

as long as I can."

"But—" He snapped his mouth shut and vaulted up the bank, hardly needing the roots at all. He leaned down and hauled up first Igraine, then Iliesa. "Come on," he called.

I pulled myself up one-handed, the other still stretched out toward the yath hound. It was pushing back, and its strength was considerable. It growled again, then looked right at me, opened its mouth and started to *eat* the spell. *Fuck.* I hadn't known that was possible. It burned along my caster's senses, an inimical force consuming my magic. I whimpered and froze, clinging to the tangle of roots, as I tried to maintain the spell. Rowan leaned down and grabbed my hand, then pulled me up as easily as he had the girls.

"Where?"

Of course. I had the disc. "The big oak," I ground out past the feel of my magic dying as it was eaten. Rowan took the disc out of my hand and slid through the underbrush to the oak. He slammed the disc into the split in the tree, and I felt the door open, silvery threads of magic visible even to the naked eye. The hound roared again.

"Run," I told the girls. They sprinted toward the oak, leaping over fallen branches and dodging around small trees.

The hound opened its maw wider than I had thought possible, and then bit through the last of my chain shield. I doubled over as the torn remnants of the spell flooded back into me. My right arm burned along the lines of my tattoo. I blinked watering eyes, and straightened to see the yath hound looming right in front of me.

"I mark you, human child." Its nostrils flared. "I have the scent of you now. My queen will know you, and when she is done, there is nowhere you can go that I will not find you."

Sometimes, there's nothing you can say. I lifted my middle finger instead.

The yath hound roared. If it was about to eat me, or take me to the queen, there wasn't much I could do about it, but I wouldn't go easily. The sidheblade pulsed against my wrist, and I envisioned a spear. Anything else would be too small against this monstrosity, and even the spear might not do much more than slow it down. But slowing it might just be enough—enough for Rowan and the girls to get away for sure, and maybe for me to go with them. I flexed my wrist and prepared to give our location away to all of Faerie.

"Kneel, child of Anand," Rowan yelled before I could call the blade into existence. "It is Danu's son who commands you."

The hound sat back in the bloody river and howled. Then it bent forward in a horrible parody of a dog who wanted to play.

Rowan grabbed my hand and yanked me to my feet. "Run," he suggested. We sprinted toward the oak. Little branches whipped at my face, and the roots which had been a helpful ladder moments before now only wanted to trip me and pitch me onto my face. We reached the oak—the girls had already gone through—and I stumbled to a stop. Silver lines pulsed and twitched around the door. Rowan drew even, took my hand, and we jumped through together. Behind us, the yath hound yowled in frustration.

We tumbled to the stone floor, and behind us the door snapped shut. The howling abruptly cut off; the silence was like a slap. I sat for a moment, bruised and scratched, my boots and jeans flaking dried blood, Rowan's fingers still clasped in my sweaty hand, my breathing very loud in the quiet room. I looked around until I saw the twins, and Hawthorn behind them, cool and elegant as always.

"My word," Hawthorn said, taking in the four of us. We were disheveled, covered in blood and mud, but she smiled at us anyway. She leaned down to talk to the girls. "You must be Morgan's nieces. Welcome to Strangehold."

*

"You didn't tell me you were the queen's son," I said.

Rowan let his hands fall open and became very involved at looking at the scars along his knuckles and wrists—reminders, I was sure, of hundreds of fights on her behalf. "I was hoping—No. I *wanted* it to be unimportant," he said after a long pause. He had bathed; his hair was still damp and fell unbraided around his shoulders to dry, and he wore a loose shirt and trousers, and no shoes.

I stood and stretched, spine popping. I too had had a shower, and the wonderful luxury of clean, unbloodied clothes, but my body was still shedding the last effects of adrenaline. "It's all right. I mean, I don't care. Ah, damn it, that's not what I mean. I'm glad you want to help me—I want to help you, too. Let me know if I can."

He nodded solemnly, as if it were a sacred vow. Maybe it was. That was all right; I meant it. "The girls will be safe here," he said. Igraine and Iliesa were in a room together, at their request. Hawthorn would have given them each their own room if they wanted it. They didn't. They were sleeping, last I'd looked in on them, after showers of their own. Luckily Strangehold seemed to have a good supply of hot water.

"Yes." I sucked on a split in my lip. I hadn't noticed when it had happened. "They can't stay here forever, though."

"Why not? It's safer than Faerie or earth, and neither plague nor the wrath of queens can find them here."

"True, but they deserve a childhood. Friends their own age. An education." I frowned. "Surely they had friends underhill, in addition to tutors."

"Maybe. I'm sure at least they had companions their own age." He looked off into the distance, moss-green eyes pensive. "But I can tell you from my own experience, nobles' children are loath to call a changeling friend, even the queen's own get."

"All the more reason to get them overhill," I said firmly, though how I was to do that with the Savannah flu still going, I didn't know. I needed to call Eliza—no. I needed to call Jake. The shock of her death hit me again like a belly blow. I rubbed my eyes, and my right bicep burned. "I'm going to go to the workroom. I need to replenish my tattoos."

"I shall accompany you." He rose to his feet with fluid grace.

"I'd appreciate that."

Everything was still set up as Marcus had left it. I

bowed my head and let myself savor the lingering feel of his magic, sharp angles and graceful arches. It might be as close as I would come to talking to him again. He was in an unbreakable trance—the polite magical way to say coma—and Hawthorn didn't think he'd come out of it. I needed to go see him, to say goodbye, but I hadn't been able to make myself do it just yet. The last image I had of him was of him blazing with magic to let us cross underhill. What I saw next would be the image that supplanted it, and I was selfish enough to want to let the other linger a little longer.

I sat cross-legged in the middle of the circle and opened myself up to the magic in the room, letting it wash over me. Silver light bathed everything in the room with a cool glow. It was more diffuse than the magic in a leyline, but it was everywhere, filtered to keep the strength of the source from ripping the caster apart. This felt the same as magic at home, and I opened myself up to it.

The stinging around my right bicep eased as magic flowed in, replacing that which I'd spent in driving back the yath hound. Though I probably ought not use it again until I repaired it. I'd need to visit the tattoo shop when I got home; the ink was faded and missing in some places where the hound had eaten it. That had never happened to me before. Rowan lent his power to mine and that indescribable thrill rippled down my spine at the feel of our combined power. I couldn't stop myself from smiling at him.

A small discordant note entered the web of my magic. I frowned and looked around, trying to spot it. Metal glinted by the fountain. Of course—Helen's bracelet. I'd forgotten all about it. I was getting better at shoving aside the sadness that came with thoughts of the dead; not a skill I'd ever wanted to cultivate. I stood and walked to the bracelet, hooking it with a finger. Some of the wards were broken past fixing, but some of them weren't; regardless, her daughter might like it as a keepsake. The wards that still functioned buzzed faintly against my skin. A silver asclepian, a rod with a snake twisted around it, caught on my sidheblade bracelet, and I pulled them apart, ignoring the tingle of the charm.

Wait. That couldn't be right. "Rowan. Look at this."

He bent to look at the bracelet. His hair fell forward; this close he smelled of rosemary. "Your friend's bangle, isn't it?"

I touched the charm with my fingertip. "This is a ward against sickness. Probably not really very helpful; there's only so much magic can do against disease." I touched the shattered quartzes. "Can you tell what these were?" He shrugged. I drew a breath. "These were wards against inimical spells."

He looked up, eyes widening. "So what killed Helen—"

"—isn't a disease at all," I finished. "It's a spell." I clenched my fist around the bracelet until the stones bit into my palm, trying to grasp the enormity of such a casting—and how anyone could actually do it.

"But it's a spell that acts like a disease," he said. "It spreads like a disease."

"Yes, or at least it seems to. Someone is a fiendish bastard. A disease might not have a cure, but most spells can be broken. Nobody else has to die." I knew that it wouldn't be that easy, but for a second I let myself believe that it might be. Relief bubbled up in me, and I grabbed his hands and spun in a circle. "I have to go back. The Association needs to know. My friend Saranya—" If she was still alive. I made myself calm down. "Let me talk to Hawthorn. If the girls can stay here while I see to this—"

"I'll come with you," he said. "Our combined knowledge might be better than yours alone." Our combined magic was stronger too, if he was willing.

*

Hawthorn was happy to let Igraine and Iliesa stay at Strangehold. The hard part was explaining to my nieces that I was leaving them again, even if I meant to come back almost before they could miss me. I came into it feeling that I was failing them already. They were all too ready to agree.

"You can't leave us here," Igraine said. Her nostrils flared as she looked around the sitting room. "We just got here."

"My dear," Hawthorn began.

"We don't mean to be rude," Iliesa cut in quickly. Igraine's chin tucked down and she glared at me through narrowed eyes.

"I don't want to go," I said. "But people are dying. If I can help them, I have to."

"You could bring us with you." Igraine's eyes darted to me.

"Only if I could swear to your parents that I could keep you safe. I'm not sure you would be." I leaned forward, willing them to be convinced. "There's a disease killing casters, and I think I can stop it. But both of you are casters too, and I haven't had a chance to put wards on you, even if I was certain this was something you could ward against. I want to teach you how to protect yourselves but right now we don't have time."

Iliesa glanced at Igraine, and Igraine slouched forward over crossed arms. "We understand," Iliesa said.

"I'll come back, and we'll have time to talk to each other." I hoped I wasn't lying to them. "I'll come back," I said again.

Iliesa nodded and held her hand out, palm up so that I could see the acorn-freckle at the center of it. "It's all right, Aunt Morgan. We trust you."

I bit my lip and hoped I'd live up to their trust.

Rowan went to gather supplies for our trip back overhill while I got the things I thought I'd need. I was almost packed when Hawthorn burst through the door of my room, her skirts held high, in the closest thing to disarray I'd seen her yet.

"Morgan! Come quickly."

I dropped my backpack on the bed and jumped up. "Is it the girls?"

"What? No, they're fine. It's Marcus. He's awake. He—he doesn't have long." She swallowed hard. "You will know when you see him."

I followed her down the corridor at a dead run, and slid through the door to his sickroom. Hawthorn hadn't lied—he looked awful. His time in the trance had left him gaunt and sallow. His breath was coming in slow, wheezing gasps, and the shadows under his eyes were bruise black. I swallowed sorrow and came to his side.

His eyes cracked open, the whites bloodshot and the eyelids rimmed with crusted black blood. The lines around them deepened in an attempt at a smile that looked more like a grimace. "You came back," he said. "Did you find them?"

"We found them. They're here. They're safe." I sat down at his bedside. "Thank you. I'd never have gotten underhill without what you did."

Marcus's gaze found mine. "Good. I'm glad. They couldn't have a better guardian than you."

"I'll do my best." I hadn't been the most promising or quickest of his pupils, but I was what the girls had.

"Your best will keep them safe." He drew in another long breath, quavering and fraught with pain.

"Can I get you anything?" I scanned the table next to his bed. There were a plethora of bottles and vials there, some the familiar orange plastic of an overhill pharmacy, some faceted crystal twined with silver vines—Hawthorn's work, or gotten from Faerie somehow.

"Hawthorn has me stuffed full of pills and potions, and Rose is blocking as much of the pain as she can. That I can feel it..." Another gasping breath. He knew as well as I that the end couldn't be far. Tears pricked my eyelids, hot and unwelcome, and I smoothed his sheet unnecessarily. "Never mind all that. I failed you."

"What? No. You were as fine a teacher as I could have wished—as anyone could have wished."

"I tried. I did try...but as your friend, I let you down."

"You helped me save my nieces. You didn't let me down, you got me to Faerie when I thought it was impossible."

"I mean twenty years ago." His eyes closed for a second, and he swallowed. "I'm sorry, Morgan. I should have stayed for you and Eliza. I shouldn't have—"

"No, Marcus. Stop. It's all right. Done is done. Eliza and I haven't done so badly for ourselves." I stilled my hand on the sheet. "You were hurting. He was your prize student." I laid my hand against his where he could grip it or not as he chose. After a long moment, he wrapped his fingers around mine. I gave him the gentlest of squeezes, letting my skin say *I'm here*. If I said it out loud, resentment might come out along with love—*and I'd have been here sooner if you'd have let me*—and I was too grateful for all he had done and too afraid this would be my last goodbye to want anything so sharp to stain it.

His eyes opened again, shining and wet with regret. "I wanted—It was so long ago when David and I—we never had children. I saw all of you as my children, I did, but Matthew—"

"—he was like your son."

"His own parents didn't know him like I did—like I thought I did. I was wrong." He turned his head to the side, a shudder wracking him. I waited, aching for him, until he turned back and dragged a faint smile up from somewhere. "Dying is terrible. Try not to do it if you can at all avoid it."

"I'll do my best." Resentment crumbled away like ash. We had both done the best we could, and both made mistakes. I leaned down and laid my lips against his forehead. "You did everything you could for us. I've always been grateful to you for it."

"I'm proud of you," he said. His eyes went distant. He fumbled for the ring at his throat, and I helped him draw it out. He closed his eyes and pain flitted like clouds across his face.

"Marcus?" I said softly. He didn't answer.

Soft footsteps brushed against the stone behind me: Hawthorn. She sat next to me for a time, and we listened to the increasingly ragged tempo of his breath. After a handful of minutes—short, objectively, but a subjective eternity—his gasps turned to a rattle, and then stopped.

The tears I'd tried not to shed in front of him fell, and Hawthorn pulled me to her side in a brief fierce embrace, a solid, comforting presence. All the deaths of the past few days and now this one—She let me weep for only a second and then pulled me up.

"You must go," she said. "I'm sorry. Leave him with us—we'll take care of him. You have to find this spell and stop it."

I wiped my eyes—not dry, because I couldn't stop crying, but drier—and nodded. I wanted to thank her, but instead I said, "Please look after him."

"Go," she said, "and come back to us."

*

There was only one door from Strangehold into Faerie, but there were dozens to Earth; the one we'd come in through, in Atlanta, ones in London, Tokyo, Sydney, Johannesburg—all over the world. The one we were taking was to New York; that was where Jake and the Association were. I didn't know if the Savannah flu had spread anywhere outside of the states yet. New York City had the highest concentration of casters on the east coast, so that's where we were headed.

Rowan and I crossed the thin vine bridge. This time I tried to look up instead of down, at the innumerable branches of the great tree that held Strangehold. It seemed lighter above us than the twilight expanse of the void below, a gentle light filtered green by all the leaves. How far did it go up? I'd have to ask Hawthorn if she'd ever walked up it. Something seemed to move in the branches, a shifting of the shadows. I stopped, hands tightening on the leafy rails. I squinted, trying to pierce the vast distance, but I couldn't see anything.

"Morgan?" Rowan had stopped too, a few feet ahead of me.

"I thought I saw something."

He looked up at the branches, brows furrowed. "I don't see anything."

"It must have been a trick of the light. Come on." I started walking again, narrowing the distance between us. He nodded, and turned back to the platform and the gate to overhill.

I had buffed both of us with all the wards of protection I knew, and Rowan had backed my wards with his power. Now that we knew it was a spell rather than a sickness, we could at least try to guard against it. If we failed—well, between Hawthorn and Rowan, I trusted the girls would be looked after. Rowan had laid a glamour over his fae features to make them look more human, and every time I looked at him, it creeped me out a little, how close to and yet not *him* his face looked.

We stepped out of Strangehold under a bridge in Central Park. The air was cold and bright, and my eyes still stung from weeping. It was late afternoon and it took me a few moments to get my bearings, but soon I had us walking to the building that housed the Association. There weren't nearly the number of people about that I'd expected to see on the streets, but considering the sickness had been on the news, probably no one was out who didn't have to be.

The Association was headquartered in an old brownstone that had been made over for commercial use. The bottom floor held a used bookstore that was almost never open. Upstairs was another matter.

The gate that guarded the stairs to the second floor was locked and warded. I sent a tendril of magic into the iron knot in the center of the window grille and waited. No one answered. I glanced at Rowan, who frowned. I sent another, stronger tendril into the knot and held it, the magical equivalent of leaning on the bell. After nearly a minute, a speaker clicked on and a brusque female voice said, "What?"

"It's Morgan Tenpenny. I'm here to see Jake Kaminski—or—or whoever's around, really." I didn't tell her that we had an idea. That's all it was—an idea. We needed to test it. It seemed all too likely we'd have more than enough test subjects.

The wards dropped, the door buzzed, and we pushed our way in.

The hallway was quiet. We walked up two flights of stairs and went through a glass door that read Allman Reed, Inc. in faded art-nouveau style letters. Shelby Allman and Philomena Reed had been the two mages who transformed the loose council of sorcerers into the organization of casters that it was today. In the lobby, a woman with a messy, bleached-blond pixie cut frowned at us from behind a desk. Bruise-purple bags shadowed her eyes. "Stop right there," she said, and I recognized her voice as the person who'd buzzed us in.

We stopped, and she looked us over, head to toe.

"Cough," she said. I met Rowan's eye, struck again by how strange he looked as a human, shrugged, and forced a cough. Rowan followed suit. She listened, her head cocked, and then nodded.

"I'm Tina Mendes. Sorry about that, but we can't have any more sick people in here."

"How bad is it?" I asked.

She looked at me, one penciled eyebrow rising up high enough to be lost in her fringe.

"We've been underhill a couple of days," I told her. The other eyebrow joined the first. "It's a long story. Is Jake here?"

"Who did you say you were?"

"Morgan Tenpenny."

She dialed a number, an old handheld set cradled between her shoulder and her ear, eyes never leaving me except to flick to Rowan. She mumbled into the phone, nodded, and set it down.

"Go on back," she said. "You know where his office

is?"

"I know where Eliza's office is."

"Then you know where his office is." She watched us, eyes narrowed, as we walked past her. Rowan stepped a little closer to me, and even amidst this grimness, I wanted to smile. Yath hounds and rivers of blood, a-okay. Grumpy receptionist, not in his wheelhouse.

I braced myself as we came to the end of the hall. I liked Jake, but it had been Eliza behind this door since we were in our late twenties—she'd been so proud of getting there so young—and I'd expected it to be her for another couple of decades at least. I swallowed hard, rapped my knuckles against the glass and waited.

The door swung open. I barely recognized Jake. He was a kid in my memory, with the slenderness of youth and the bulk of someone who hit the weights on a regular basis. But now, his face was haggard, his eyes were rimmed with red, and he had dropped maybe ten pounds that he didn't have to spare. He hooked an elbow in front of his face and coughed.

"Sorry," he gasped. I *heard* the phlegm in his voice, thick and rumbling.

"We have an idea about how to treat this," I said without preamble.

"You're..." He sucked in a cautious breath to keep himself from coughing. "...not a doctor."

"I know. But Jake, this isn't a disease. It's a spell."

His fingers clenched, and he waved us to a seat by Eliza's—by his desk. "How do you know?"

I pulled the bracelet from my pocket and held it in the

flat of my palm. "I found this at Helen Oshiro's house. Look." I told him about Helen's house, showed him the intact ward against disease and the shattered wards against dangerous spells. "I know Saranya would be the better person to consult if this really was a disease," I finished. "But I'm pretty sure it's not, and I'm what you've got."

He nodded slowly, and raised bloodshot eyes to meet mine. "All right, you've got your first case." He spread his arms wide. "Go to town."

Now was as good a time as any. I rolled my shoulders back, enjoyed the sound of my spine popping, and summoned the silvery layer of spellsight to take a closer look. I had only looked at Helen for a moment, repulsed by the burrowing spell lines, afraid of infection—and that was certainly still a risk; just because this wasn't a disease *per se* didn't mean it couldn't kill me—but now I believed that I could figure it out, and that belief made all the difference. As I had seen in Helen, silver worms of his own magic writhed in and out of Jake's body. My instinct was to flinch away, but I made myself look at what they were doing. That they were attacking his lymph nodes was obvious, but I looked closer.

Strands of silver wrapped through the flow of magic through his body. Usually the magic of one's own body stayed beneath the skin, layered in blood and bone. What the worms were doing to him was beyond me, but they dipped in and out of him. They didn't seem inclined to come out of his body, even when I put my hand directly in their path, ignoring Rowan's faint hiss at my recklessness. With my caster's sight trained on Jake, I sifted through the rush of magic. I wanted to trace the worms to their source. I searched from the follicles of his head to the nails on his toes, and everything in between. On my second slow pass, I saw it.

Lodged in the flow of energy from his heart was an infinitesimally tiny knot. My lips stung as the blood fled from my extremities, seeking solace in my own heart. I knew this knot, as intimately as I had known Eliza's magic. It was derived from Marcus's teaching, but tailored over time to its caster. I had never thought to see it again. *Matthew*.

I chased the silver-thread ends of the knot and started patiently unpicking. There was no use rushing—that would only pull it tighter, and make Jake sicker. I could see where I needed to go; it was just a question of taking my time to get there so I didn't hurt him. Worse than the knot itself was the cold anger frozen in my chest. I would have to retrace the trail of the knot—if I could—but I already had my suspicions, and they felt like certainties.

Rowan had boosted my power at Helen's house, and I had drawn off Strangehold's energy after that. Every other poor bastard had drawn magic from a leyline.

The last thread holding the knot together dissolved. The silver lines wriggling through Jake fell away. As that power released him, he reached instinctively for the leylines.

"Stop!" I said. Jake and Rowan both looked at me. "Don't use the leylines," I said. "It's a spell, right, but it's been spreading like a disease. What if the vector of transmission is the leylines?"

Jake swore, and it turned into a cough. He already looked better—his face less haggard, his eyes less red—but it would take time for him to heal. "We have to spread the word," he said. "I have to tell everyone—"

"Yes," I said. "They have to know. No one can use the leylines until we figure this out. Who's still healthy that can help me with the sick people? Are they here, or are they in hospitals?"

"Tina," he said immediately. "There are a few other healthy people here. You need to help Saranya next. Eliza—" His face crumpled, but then he shook his head and kept going. "Eliza called her here early on. We've set up some of the apartments upstairs as sick rooms, but she can get in to the hospitals to help the people who are there."

"Right." I glanced at Rowan, who nodded.

"I'll help as long as I can," he said quietly, and glanced toward the window.

The next several hours were not pleasant ones. With every knot I untied, I grew more certain, and angrier. Rowan helped me for a while, but as the sun set, he murmured an excuse to Jake and left to undertake his transformation somewhere private. I kept going. I drained my tattoos dry, until I felt limp as a wet handkerchief and a headache pulsed around my temples. Jake brought me some objects of power that had been stored in the Association's attics, and I pulled those dry as well. It was crippling to be unable to use the leylines, and I reached out to them automatically and had to pull myself back a dozen times.

Saranya was the first person I—healed was the wrong word; broke the spell on—after Jake. She rested, watching, for perhaps an hour, as I untied the knots on the next four people. Then she helped me until she could see what to do. Jake sent Tina to the vaults for more magical artifacts we could drain. Saranya left after a while, taking some with her, headed to the closest hospital. She needed to rest, but I didn't try to stop her. We both knew people would die if we delayed.

By midnight, every sick person in the Association building was at least free from the knot and on the mend, though only time would truly bring healing, and I was starving, exhausted, and my head pounded. Jake had been watching me work, and had felt well enough to help with the last few. I was confident that he could un-knot sufferers himself, and show other people how to do it. The problem now was that we were running out of artifacts to drain, and we couldn't use the leylines until we were sure they were safe. I'd even drained the remaining charms on Helen's bracelet. I couldn't think that she'd have minded.

We sat down to peanut butter sandwiches, and in my case a couple of ibuprofen. I rubbed the skin beneath my eyes. It felt puffy. Jake was looking better than he had been, but neither of us were in great shape.

"Do you think we'll be able to find anything else to drain tomorrow?"

Jake nodded, half-staring into the distance, maybe running down some mental inventory. "It won't be enough," he said, "but it'll be something. I'll put a call out, see if anyone can donate from their personal collections."

"I'm going to Savannah," I said. "If this started there, then maybe we can stop it there. If this *does* originate in the leyline, and we can clear it, then we'll be able to help people that much faster. I can be there tomorrow."

"That's a long trip," Jake said. "You need to sleep at some point."

"I can sleep on the plane," I lied. Going through Strangehold could get me there fastest, but I couldn't tell Jake about it. It was Hawthorn's place to reveal it—or Rose's, I supposed.

He set his half-eaten sandwich down and rubbed his eyes. "When we thought this was a disease, that was bad enough, but if it's a spell, someone set it." His bloodshot eyes searched my face. "Do you know who did this?"

My own appetite had fled, but he had to know. This was a secret I didn't need to keep—shouldn't keep. If I ran into trouble looking for the source of the spell, then someone else would have to follow through. "Eliza and I were apprenticed to Marcus Grey at the same time. The other student was called Matthew March." Jake's eyes widened. "Of course you've heard of him. Well, when he was exiled, they sent him to a little island off South Carolina, which is—"

"Not far from Savannah." He bit his lower lip. "Eliza told me about him. But this is all supposition."

"Not all." I took a swallow of tepid, bitter coffee. "I worked with him as a student enough to recognize the way he casts. I'm pretty sure the knot is his work. It's why I think he used the leyine. He can't set foot on the mainland, but he could do something to the leyline where it follows the river."

"Why would he do this?"

"I don't know. It's been almost twenty years since I saw him, and I never knew him as well as I thought I did. At a guess, I'd say he's pissed about being exiled."

Jake let his head fall forward and rest on his forearms. "Do you really think you can find what he did?"

"Only one way to find out." I massaged my temples. The headache was beginning to recede. "If I don't come back, send Saranya, yes? I think she's seen his spells before."

"Come back, Morgan." He attempted a smile. "Someone's going to have to help me refill all the stuff we've drained."

So right after dawn, after far too little sleep, Rowan and I retraced our steps to the bridge in Central Park, and from there to Strangehold.

We barely took the time to say hello to the twins and Hawthorn. I explained the situation as best I could while refilling my tattoos in the workroom, the easy flow of power a luxury after New York, aware that the words were tumbling out too fast. Rowan interjected here and there to clarify a point. When I was done, Hawthorn stood and started to pace.

"Abominable," she said. "Simply abominable. Of course you must find the source of it and stop it. And I must help as I may. No, Rose," she addressed the air. "It isn't to be thought of. I will simply go disguised. I shall be perfectly safe. The queen is unlikely to send forth her minions when she has shut the gates underhill so thoroughly. You say this young man Jake is the person I ought to contact?"

"No," I said. "I mean, you can, but if you can find Dr. Saranya Ramachandran, she could best direct you. We will all truly appreciate your help."

"Pish tosh," she said. "I would have to be made of stone to ignore such dire need when I could help. You young ladies will have to look after Rose for me until I get back," she said to Igraine and Iliesa.

"We will," said Igraine, and they both nodded.

"I like her," Iliesa added softly.

"And she likes you." Hawthorn smiled. "Well. Let me gather my things. Good luck, Morgan. I hope you clear the leyline of this contamination with all possible haste."

"Me too," I muttered.

*

The drive from Atlanta to Savannah is boring. Once you pass Macon, there's miles and miles of nothing much but farms—and I say that as someone who lived in the middle of nothing much but farms. The highway was straight and flat and went on and on, interrupted only by the occasional gas station or restaurant. We stopped at one of the former to gas up and get coffee—we weren't quite on empty yet, but it was a long way between gas stations. I'd had to pay an exorbitant fee to get the truck out of parking in Atlanta, but at least it let me know how long we'd been in Strangehold and Faerie: five days. How many people had died in that time?

Savannah came up suddenly after hours of driving; a couple of billboards gave warning of restaurants and beaches ahead, and then buildings appeared where there had only been trees. From the highway it wasn't far to the river, past brick buildings. We parked by River Street. The street was almost empty, and a lot of the stores were closed. I bought a map at a shop full of tourist crap from a man wearing a surgical mask and blue latex gloves. We sat on a bench and looked at the map.

"The biggest leyline follows the river for a while, so it makes sense that whatever he did is somewhere along the river." I followed the map with my finger. The river was interrupted by several islands, Tybee Island being the biggest. "He was exiled never to set foot on the mainland, so I don't think we'll find it here. I think we'll find it somewhere along here." I traced the coast of Tybee with my finger.

"What's this?" Rowan leaned over the map, examining a little x marking a spot.

"That's the lighthouse," I said. The lighthouse stood on the farthest point out toward open water. If one were cursed not to set foot on the mainland and concerned about exactly where that curse kicked in, this looked like the least risky place to try. It was a start, anyway.

"There's a feygate close by." Rowan tapped the map. "Right here where the leyline and the river run apace."

"Where the leyline first crosses the coastline."

We exchanged a look, then I stood and pulled him to his feet after me.

It was a pretty drive, at least. There were great oaks dripping with Spanish moss, beautiful old buildings, some restored to former grandeur, some dilapidated, waterways with a few boats moored along piers, and a seemingly endless sea of reeds. A looming feeling of dread hung over me, though; not a presentiment of failure, exactly, but a fear of what we'd find where the land met the water. I had a hunch we had the right spot. I couldn't reconcile a man who would spread this plague with the man I had known twenty years before, but then, I hadn't understood the attack that got him exiled, either.

A memory: Matthew and I cataloging items in the Association storage, aka the attic. It had been a brilliant day early in September. The attics were stuffy and dusty. We'd propped open a window, and the occasional puff of outside air cooled my sweaty skin. Marcus and Eliza had gone to pick up lunch, and Matthew and I were still working desultorily while we waited for them to come back.

Matthew was scrying some of the uncatalogued items—showing off; he was much better at scrying than me, and could tell whether they were magic or just junk, and even pick up some of the history of the things. I had a ballpoint pen and a printout on dot matrix paper to match to each item. I was peeling off the perforated edges when Matthew's voice floated out from behind a box in the corner of the attic.

"Oh ho, what's this?" He came out, holding a long gilt box tied with what appeared to be a piece of velvet theater curtain, faded along the top where sunlight had bleached it.

I ran the cap of my pen down my list and stopped at *one decorative silver dagger in a gold box*. "I have a guess, but let's open it and see. You have a cobweb in your hair."

He set the box by my feet and ran his hands briskly through his hair. "As long as I don't have the cob, I'll be all right." He tugged at the velvet tie and pried the lid off the box. A silver dagger gleamed against more velvet. Matthew sent a tentative tendril of magic to it, and it roared to life, energy humming through it. It was years until I would have my own sidheblade, but I knew what it was. Matthew did too; his face tightened with surprise. "What's it doing wasted up here?" he said.

"Well, since the peace, I guess no one's gone hunting the fae." Sidheblades were made of silver from Faerie and forged by fae smiths who imbued them with spells so that they changed shape according to their wielders' need. Cold iron remained the best way to really ruin a fae's day, but sidheblades were a close second, and much easier to hide; when they were inert, they didn't show up to fae sight the way cold iron did. Until a sidheblade changed into a sword or spear or whatever, it looked like normal silver. A few of them had been gifted to favored humans and a few of them had been stolen, but they were very rare overhill. I wondered how long this one had been miscataloged and forgotten. "We'll have to tell Marcus about it."

"I'll do it," Matthew said casually, and dropped the lid back on the box. "I never thought I'd see one—wish we could put it in a museum." He smiled, and I put a tick next to the line on my printout. We started looking for the next thing, a silver chalice of unknown origin, and I'd forgotten the exchange until much, much later, when Matthew stabbed the queen's nephew with the stolen sidheblade.

Tybee Island was beautiful and empty. We parked beside a white sand beach gleaming gold in the afternoon sun. The lighthouse loomed over the sand, an angular building painted black and white. I walked to the water, then turned back and looked at the lighthouse. I let my vision blur and brought forward my spellsight. Lines of silver fell like vines creeping toward the leyline—from the top of the lighthouse tower. The uneasy feeling I'd had in the car returned.

"Do you see?" Rowan asked quietly.

I nodded. We walked together around the base of the lighthouse until we found the door. According to the signs, there were ordinarily tours of the lighthouse, but the lighthouse and its accompanying museum were closed indefinitely, I presumed due to sickness. I looked around, but there was no one about but us; even the little restaurant by the beach was closed.

The door was locked, but a small twist of energy from the tattoo at my shoulder opened it. We slipped in and started ascending. We walked up and up, until my legs ached and my panting breath echoed in the small spiral stairway. Landings and windows broke up the climb, welcome both for a moment of flat walking, and for the cooling breeze.

Power concentrated around us as we walked, and I *felt* we were getting closer to some spell, even if it were not Matthew's. Finally, we reached the top. Rowan looked at me, and we walked in, me first and him right behind me.

I hadn't expected it to be so bright, but the whole top of the lighthouse was glass. There was a metal walkway around the outside of the building. I had a momentary impression of miles and miles of sea, but then I saw Matthew, and my focus narrowed entirely to him.

He was slumped against one glass wall, smiling sardonically. He was thinner than I remembered, and of course older. A web of silver energy wove in front of him, hiding him from non-magical eyes. Behind him a thick strand of silvery light went through the tower walls to the leyline below. He had tied *himself* into the spell. I had wondered how the spell continued to renew itself, sending knot after knot into the leyline—now I knew. He was draining his life to do it. He had always been so clever, and this was how he chose to waste that gift? Bile rose in my throat.

"Matthew, what have you done?"

I had barely breathed it, but he looked up and his eyes widened.

"Morgan? I thought they would send Eliza." He laughed, a horrible creaking sound.

"Eliza's dead. Your little trick killed her, along with a lot of other people."

He shoved himself up against the wall. "What are you talking about?"

Had he driven himself mad, tied to this spell? "The knots you're sending down the leyline. Congratulations. You've revenged yourself on everyone for exiling you. Hundreds of people are dead."

"No...you're lying." His face twisted into a terrible rictus.

"Why the hell would I lie to you about this? People are dying."

He laughed again, a choked, bitter sound. "Impossible. The spell was set for the feygate. It could never have gotten past it to the main artery of the leyline. It's been destroying our enemies."

"It's been destroying *us*. It never made it to the feygate."

Rowan stepped out from behind me into the room. Matthew's face contorted again and he exhaled a hissing breath.

"You're wrong." Rowan's voice was calm and even. "The queen closed the feygates, and your work bypassed Faerie and turned against your own people."

Matthew's eyes closed. "No. That's impossible."

Matthew had killed hundreds. Maybe he'd been aiming for genocide, or just to take out as many as he could before the fae stopped the spell. But he must have known he couldn't kill every single fae, and those who'd been left would have retaliated. "What did you hope to accomplish?"

"They prey on us," Matthew said. "They never keep their promises. This flimsy peace won't last and when it breaks, we'll be nothing more than an amusement to them as we die. As it has been, so will it be. How many have we lost to them, over the centuries?"

"Is it more or less than we've lost to you in the last week?" I snapped.

"You keep saying it, but I don't believe you." He sighed. It sounded painful, and I couldn't be sorry. "I can't believe you're here with one of *them*."

"You're the problem here, Matthew, not me." I tried to think of what I could say to him to convince him. I jammed my hands in my pockets, and then realized I didn't need to say anything. I hooked a finger around the chain of Helen's bracelet and slid it out of my pocket. I held it up and he started at it blankly. Of course it meant nothing to him. He hadn't known Helen.

"What's this?"

I took his hand and closed his fingers around the spent charms. "Scry it," I said. "You'll see the death of its owner. You'll see where I took the energy from the charms while Eliza's deputy and I tried to counter your spell. I was able to recognize the knots of your work—surely you'll be able to." My voice didn't waver. I was proud of that.

It was a long second before he turned his gaze from my eyes to the bracelet, but he did. His eyes unfocused as he sent a tendril of power into the bracelet and read its recent history. His eyes shone—with horror, I thought. "Oh, God," he muttered. His focus returned, and he shook his head, refusing to look at me. "I never meant to—Morgan. You have to tell them. I didn't mean to do this. I would never—"

"But you did."

"I can't make this right," he said.

"But you can end it," I said softly.

Rowan looked at him, and then turned to me. "There's an obvious solution." he said. "This man's life is holding the spell together. Eliminate one, and the other will dissipate."

Matthew flinched, and turned his head toward the leyline. "I can't stop the spell," he said. "It's got too much of me in it, too much momentum. He's right. The only way it ends is when I die." His gaze turned back toward me. "Please. My family—they're on Loblolly Island."

"I'll find them," I promised. I hadn't even known he had a family. If they had helped him in this, the council would judge them. And if they hadn't, we would help them.

He smiled, and for a moment, he looked like the man I had known twenty years before. He closed his eyes, and a faint spark of magic brought a swirl of silver over his heart. I could already see it wouldn't be enough.

"I can't." He looked directly at me, his eyes wet. "I can't pull enough magic from the spell."

"Then I will do it for you." Rowan drew a dagger from his belt. It glinted dangerously in the sunlight.

"No!" Matthew scrabbled backward reflexively, though with his back against the wall he didn't get far. "No. I want a human death." He looked at me.

God damn it, Matthew. I'd been in fights before over the course of my career as a caster, but I'd never killed anyone, or ever thought I would have to. I wasn't especially eager to begin my career as a murderer.

"Morgan," Rowan murmured. "There is no need. My hands are long since stained red. Let me bear this burden."

Matthew's eyes widened. His power surged forward and he barely caught it. "No. I swear it, I will send my dying energy into this spell. Don't let him touch me!"

Every second we spent dithering here was another second he might be killing innocents. "Calm yourself, Matthew. I'll do it."

Rowan's mouth went flat and thin-lipped, but I ignored him. Blood rushed in my ears, and my pulse sped until I felt lightheaded. I couldn't bear the thought of killing him with magic—letting my energy twist with his and then killing him with it. It would be horribly intimate. I didn't want to share that much with him. I called to the silver bracelet on my wrist and let the sidheblade fall into existence as a dagger with a razor-sharp edge.

Power crackled as it manifested, bending the flow of the silver lines that spellsight showed throughout the room. Rowan and Matthew both flinched away.

"Is that—" Matthew gasped.

"No," I said. "The queen took that one. I found this one later." Rowan glanced at the dagger and frowned.

The weight of the blade steadied my shaking hands. Everything seemed unreal, like a scene from a movie. I couldn't possibly be considering killing a man, *this* man, who had once been my friend, and yet...because of him, Helen and Eliza and countless others were dead. If Gwen was dead or tortured, I could lay that at his feet too: the queen of Faerie would have left Gwen and Elm alone but for his actions.

I rolled my shoulders and fell into a ready stance, and tried to make myself step toward him. One step. Two. The sidheblade didn't share my reservations; I could feel its hunger, and I let it draw me forward.

Matthew bowed his head. I raised the sidheblade to strike.

Rowan darted forward, quick as a falcon diving, and slid a wide dagger across Matthew's throat. The slice was fast and deep, and the edge so keen it took a second for the blood to spurt out. Matthew tried to take a breath, frowned, and then pitched forward to the floor. I lowered the sidheblade, sickened, as blood began to pool beneath him. The energy he had poured his life into dissipated, floating away in drifting silver filaments.

I let the sidheblade retreat to its bracelet, and drew in a hitching breath. I was shaking and I couldn't seem to stop. A puddle of blood on the floor looks different than a river of blood, it turns out. For one thing, there's the body it's coming from. Matthew's eyes were open, staring. He already looked like a bad copy of himself.

Rowan dropped to one knee next to the body and bent his head. Red-brown hair had come free from where he'd tied it back, and it fell forward into his face as he murmured something. He finished, stood, and wiped the blade on Matthew's shirt. Then he frowned, and the leyline's power *bent* toward him.

Matthew went up in blinding white flames that burned with no smoke. I heard sickening pops and cracks, and then the flame incandesced, and he was gone without so much as a scent of char to mark his passing. The flame followed the puddle of blood as if it were gasoline, and then that too was gone. It was if the last fifteen minutes had never happened, as if we had never seen Matthew, never killed him. As if he had never been here at all.

"How did you...?" The floor wasn't marked with so much as a smudge. I couldn't quit staring at it.

"Salamander," he said succinctly. They lived in the leylines near volcanoes and hot springs, but there were none that I knew of on the east coast. Another mystery, but at the moment I couldn't bring myself to care how he'd done it.

I made myself look at him. He was the same as ever, maybe a little more disheveled than usual. I had known he had been the Queen's Blade, but I hadn't *known* it, not in the bones of understanding. Well, I did now. I couldn't unsee that perfect, precise slash, delivered with deadly grace born of unimaginable practice. I didn't know how I felt. I was relieved I hadn't had to kill Matthew after all, angry that Rowan had taken the risk Matthew would end his life contaminating the leylines further, weirdly indignant—as much as I didn't *want* to have taken a life, I also was pissed that he might have thought me too cowardly or weak or whatever to have done it—and uncomfortable with my new awareness of Rowan's deadliness. Which one would surface as strongest was up for debate, but for now, I had to acknowledge the relief.

I caught his eye and forced myself to hold his gaze. His eyes were that vivid, unnatural green again. "Thank you," I said awkwardly. "I really didn't want to kill him."

"You are welcome. I...didn't want you to have to..." He looked away first. "We should not linger here."

We walked down the interminable stairs—away, I couldn't help thinking, from the scene of the crime—until we reached the bottom: the chained-in walkways, the white sand beach. One more layer of dissonance between what we had done and reality.

I pulled my phone from my pocket and hit Eliza's number on speed dial. Jake answered.

"It's done," I said, before he could say anything. "Please tell me it worked."

"I have watchers along the leylines to the southeast," Jake said. "It'll probably take a few days to know for sure." I blew out air in a wordless and inarticulate sound of frustration. "It's all right," he went on. "Your friend Jane came to help."

"Jane?" I had no idea who he meant.

"Jane Hawthorn. We've been making sure people are okay. Saranya's fine," he added. "She's taking care of Atlanta."

My knees buckled—which was something I'd heard of but never experienced, and it was an unpleasant sensation—and Rowan put a hand out to steady me. I sagged against him before I could stop myself, or decide if I wanted to.

"We'll be there as soon as we can."

"Get some rest," Jake said. "You won't be able to help anyone if you fall on your face, or wreck on the way back."

We said our goodbyes—I couldn't bear to ask after anyone specifically in case I was asking about someone dead—and I stood for a moment, letting the sun soak into me. I wanted to do as Jake said. I was so tired, and I wanted some time to think, to react to what I'd seen and done, and almost done. We had prevented more deaths, but we'd had to kill someone to do it. That it was what the Association would have done if he'd been tried was no comfort to me. Hell, we could have put him in the truck and driven him onto the mainland if only we could have moved him from the spell—he'd have been just as dead, and no one would have had to kill him. Part of me was mad at Matthew for not having the magic to kill himself. It wasn't as big a part as the one wondering how he'd gotten to the point of attempted genocide in the first place. I rubbed my face with both hands. My eyes ached.

Rowan let his hand fall away and I gave myself a

moment to regret the loss. "Back to Strangehold?"

"Not quite yet. We have one more thing to do."

*

Loblolly Island was hard to find, unless you were a caster. Very specific, very local maps used to show it to the east of Fripp Island, but since Matthew had been exiled to it, no one without magic could find so much as a trace of it, either on a map or in person. As it was now, a person without magic would boat right by it, and a caster would feel the council's alarms buzzing against their skin.

The motor of our boat sputtered behind us, propelling us though weed-choked lanes. We had driven a little over an hour to Fripp and then rented a boat from a resident; Fripp was supposed to be the easternmost island. Nothing more than a thin slice of sea separated Loblolly Island from Fripp Island, but unless there was another caster on Fripp, no one but us could see it.

Loblolly was less than two square miles, so it didn't take us long to find the pier that jutted into the water between the two islands. "They'll probably be afraid of you," I told Rowan on the drive, "because Matthew won't have been shy about his views. Let me do the talking." He laughed—an honest sound I wanted to drink in, because the drive had been mostly awkward silence—and pulled up his human glamour.

I went first up the dirt track from the rickety pier to the house. It had been not much more than a shack when the council first brought Matthew here. In the intervening decades, the shack had become a house and a few outbuildings—enough to make me wonder just how big his family was. Chickens wandered around the yard, pecking desultorily in the grass. A lone goat came close and watched us hopefully, *maaaaa*ing intently when we didn't pay it enough attention.

My shoulders rose around my ears as we drew closer. It took me a second to realize why—the buzzing of flies crescendoed as we drew away from the pier. That might have just been bugs along the mud, but it got louder as we got closer to the house. I made a fist, nails digging into my palms, and looked at Rowan. His eyes narrowed, and his hand rested easily on the dagger he had wielded so efficiently earlier.

I braced myself and pushed on the front door. It didn't have a lock—why would they need one?

The smell wafted out, along with a wave of flies. I gagged and stumbled backward. Rowan offered a handkerchief, which I pressed to my nose. It smelled faintly of rosemary and lime, and it didn't help much, but it was better than nothing.

There were two people inside, a woman and a man. They looked to be of Hispanic descent. Matthew had called them his family. I wondered if one of them was his spouse or lover, and who the other was. How could the Savannah flu have possibly killed them? The leylines flowed inland. Then my brain processed what I was seeing: each corpse bore a small spot of blood staining their shirts in the middle of the chest.

Rowan bent forward and examined them, holding another over his own nose. It mostly hid his expression, but when he straightened, his eyebrows were drawn together in a troubled vee.

"A precise strike," he said. "Straight to the heart. They died within seconds."

"At least they didn't suffer." I tried to keep my voice steady, but it was difficult. Matthew had not done this. These were his family, and he had thought them alive in his last moments of life. Who had known they were here? Who had known that he was involved? It would be stretching coincidence to the breaking point to assume that these deaths were unrelated to Matthew's actions. "Should we bury them? Or..." I swallowed. "The council will probably want to see them, to find who did this. I suppose we shouldn't disturb the evidence."

"There is no need." Rowan's voice was nearly a growl. "I know who the perpetrator was, or *what* he was, anyway." His hand fell from his face. He had dropped the human glamour. I couldn't read his expression; nor did I really want to. "When her majesty wished to destroy the associates of someone she wanted to punish, I was often ordered to kill with a single strike to the heart—if they were guilty of nothing more than association. It was a kind of mercy, that they not suffer. The queen has named a new Blade."

*

I had just begun to summon the energy to cast a preservation spell when Rowan called the salamander back and set the house and the pitiful corpses within ablaze. I yelled at him about destroying the evidence, he yelled back about potential nasties the new Blade might have left on the body, and as a result, the boat ride back to the mainland was somewhat frostier than the ride out had been. I kept trying to call Jake but it was a while before I had reception.

"What now?" Rowan asked, his voice still somewhat guarded, after I slipped my phone into my pocket after the latest attempt. I rubbed my eyes.

"Back to Strangehold and the girls. Saranya and Jake might need my help undoing Matthew's work, but he's right—I won't be much good to them without some rest, and a chance to—" Let myself give into shock? Mourn a monster who'd caused the death of who knew how many people, while at the same time mourning those people? "—process everything. And try to get in touch with Gwen or Elm."

His expression softened. "Perhaps I will be able to help with the latter."

"Thank you." I couldn't bring myself to apologize for yelling at him when I still thought I was right, but at least we were talking to each other politely.

So the drive to Atlanta wasn't as dire as it could have been, besides being long and tedious. We hit Macon right before sunset and got something to eat just in time. We walked behind a gas station and watched the sun inching below the horizon. "I hate this," he said conversationally.

"I'm sorry," I said. "Is there a way out of it?" I was curious about the terms of Rowan's transformation but I didn't want to offend him or pry if he didn't want to tell me.

"There's always a way out, Morgan." But whether he would have told me or not then, the sun fell behind the tree line, and in that instant, the man was gone and the falcon was there. He called once, then flew to the truck and perched on the cab, waiting for me.

*

Strangehold was comfortingly familiar in its weirdness. It was funny how crossing a narrow bridge over an abyss to a tree fortress in the source of magic could feel like a homecoming—but some of that was due to who was waiting on the other end.

I told Hawthorn and the twins almost everything—that there had been a man who tried to attack Faerie and failed, that the human sickness was over. That we could go home. I left out how Matthew had died, and what we had found at his house. I didn't mention Rowan's suspicion that there was a new Queen's Blade. And that the queen had used the new Blade against a human, breaking one of the terms of the treaty. I'd have to tell Jake. Hawthorn's eyes darted to Rowan, but if he wanted to tell her what I was omitting, he could do it later. I didn't really want to talk about it. Not when I had other things to focus on.

Rowan and Hawthorn tactfully excused themselves, and I was alone with my nieces. Iliesa watched them leave, while Igraine stared directly at me.

"We don't want to leave," she blurted as soon as the door was closed. "Hawthorn said we could stay as long as we liked, but she said you would want to take us overhill. We want to stay here."

"The dragons are nice," Igraine added.

"The dragons?" I hesitated. There were no dragons on earth or in Faerie. Could they exist in Strangehold? I needed to ask Hawthorn.

"There's no such thing as dragons," Iliesa said testily.

"We want to stay here." She sat down next to Igraine and took her hand. We were in one of Strangehold's sitting rooms. Hawthorn had brought us tea and petit fours that I hadn't had the appetite to touch. I poured myself a cup of tea now, to give myself a moment to think. I hadn't expected this reaction, though maybe I should have. Leaving Faerie had been frightening, and they were safe here. Why wouldn't they want to stay?

"There are a couple of reasons why we can't." A huge one was that at home I had contacts and magical resources to look for Gwen, but I didn't want to bring that up immediately. "Your education is important—both your magical education and your mundane education. You should learn how to use the human half of your magic—in the human world, not just here at Strangehold. You can go to school, and make friends your own age."

"We won't be there long enough to make friends," Igraine snapped. "Our parents will come take us home before we have time for that."

I took a sip of tea. "I hope so. But your mother asked me to take care of you even before she was—" I searched for a word. "—detained. Faerie isn't safe for your family right now. Even if they're both home right now, they asked me to take care of you for now, and the best way I can do that is by taking you home. To my home."

Iliesa turned her head away, but not before I saw the sheen to her eyes. "But what if we hate it there?"

"If you give it a chance and still hate it, we'll figure something else. Overhill is a big place, bigger than underhill. If you don't like my particular piece of it, we can go somewhere else."

Igraine shot me a look, but she didn't seem as hostile. "We really could go somewhere else?"

"I want you to be happy," I said. "We won't stay away from Strangehold forever. We can visit Hawthorn whenever you want." A pang shot through my heart for Marcus. I swallowed that grief; the girls had enough of their own.

"Do you think they might be home right now?" Iliesa probably didn't believe it any more than I did, but her eyes begged me to lie to her.

"I don't know," I said instead. "I hope so. We'll do whatever we can to find out, and if they're not, we'll do whatever we can to find them."

"How much can you do?" Igraine's tone was scornful, but I thought she wanted reassurance as much as her sister did.

I called energy from Strangehold into me and sent it into the oak tree tattooed on my chest. I was prepared to have to wrestle it to use it, but it was as gentle as a comforting hand. My eyes itched with wanting to close and I ached all over; not just physically, but emotionally. I wanted to let myself fall apart, but they needed me to show them that I could help. The pair of tiny acorns emblazoned on my skin pulsed with life, and I sent energy along the threads that bound me to the girls. They both looked at me, eyebrows raised.

"Your mother asked me to promise to protect you and I did. I never marked her as I did you, but it doesn't mean I don't have ways of finding her, and I know people who will help. I promise you I will do everything I can to find her." I let the magic drain out of the link to them.

They looked at each other, and without speaking seemed to have a conversation. I hoped they would eventually trust me enough to let me in. "We'll go with you," Iliesa said. My shoulders unknotted and I smiled tentatively at them.

"We'll go in the morning," I began, already calculating what I'd need to do to get them settled.

A noise at the door made us all turn. Rowan and Hawthorn stood, framed perfectly by the doorframe. Rowan had cleared his throat. "They feygates are open once more," Hawthorn announced. Her eyes sparkled. "I gave young Jakub some advice about the best approach to take with the queen," she added modestly. "His message must have been well received."

Rowan met my eyes, and I found it hard to hold his gaze. I had seen him kill, and I still wasn't sure how I felt about that. "I'm returning to Faerie," he said.

"Oh," I said. "You have to do what you need to, of course."

He turned to the girls, who met his eyes with no hesitation. Lucky girls. "If what happened to your parents is known, I will find out, and I'll tell you."

"We're going back overhill tomorrow." I glanced at the twins, who nodded.

"I'll find you," he said.

"And you are welcome here whenever you like," Hawthorn said brightly. "Rose and I would both think it splendid to see you again." She cocked her head to one side. "Rose has a thought—if you like, we could build a door from overhill somewhat closer to you to make visiting easier."

The girls lit up, and I leaned forward, liking the thought, with a few ideas of where we might put the door. By the time I looked to Rowan, he was gone.

*

Three weeks later, the twins were settled in my second bedroom and a week into a so-far positive experience overhill. We'd spent a little time in a crash course in modern technology, but for people who'd never seen a cell phone before, they figured out the internet and video games pretty quickly. Then again, they were eleven. I requested the paperwork to get them enrolled in the local school, and downloaded reams of syllabi to figure out what they should already know by the time they got there to see what gaps in their education we'd need to fill in before they started.

They had worked with me to make a door to Strangehold in the old stone bridge over the creek behind my house. Hawthorn and Rose had activated it the week before, and we had visited Strangehold. Only yesterday, Hawthorn had come to visit for the first time and the girls had shown her their room, the cats that visited from the woods, the network of wards I had been putting up ever since we came home. If the fae lady felt as incongruous as she looked taking tea out of a Wonder Woman mug, she didn't show it. Both girls had been interested in what I could show them of human magic. If Igraine was occasionally snappy and Iliesa occasionally mopey, I figured they deserved to be.

And I wasn't any different, really; I was just older and

better at keeping snappy and mopey to myself.

Sometimes after they were asleep I would sit in my kitchen and think about everyone I'd lost in the last few weeks—Eliza, Marcus, and Helen were only the ones I was closest to. And then there was Gwen, whose loss I refused to accept. I was still finding out that casters I'd known were gone when I'd try to get in touch with them, or mention them to someone else. In the end, the death toll for the Savannah flu had numbered in the hundreds: enough to send the whole US into a panic and shut down flights to other countries, enough to generate a Wikipedia article. But less than a month later, the news had mostly moved on and the general populace could let it go. But for the magical populace, it was a devastating blow. I didn't know exactly how many casters there were in the US, but hundreds was a chunk of us. We'd had our own little apocalypse, and no one else had noticed.

The world went on.

It was enough to make me want to start drinking and not stop, but I didn't. I might have if I'd been by myself, but there were the twins. I still hadn't found out anything about their parents. None of my spells had yielded anything useful yet. The eight ball kept coming up "reply hazy, ask again later." I kept asking, but every time I had to ask again, my hope dimmed a little.

It was almost dawn, and I was outside, tracing the leylines that surrounded my house. I wondered if I would ever lose the elevated heart rate, mouth-drying fear that filled me as I checked the flow of energy. I did it morning and night, and before the girls' daily lesson in magic. The silver tracery of magic flowed peacefully under a gibbous moon fading as the rising sun pinked the horizon. There was nothing there; it was fine. But still, I looked for anything anomalous, another attack from someone like Matthew.

An owl called from somewhere in the woods on its way home from the hunt. I rolled my shoulders and rubbed my eyes. I hadn't had enough sleep, but that was par for the course. I hadn't been able to stay asleep for more than a few hours at a time since we came home. When I did sleep, dreams catapulted me into an itchy wakefulness, pulse speeding, mouth dry.

The first rays of the sun slipped over the treetops, edging the dark pine with gold. I turned back toward the house, thinking only of the coffee waiting there.

The silver network of magic rippled gently. I called energy to my freshly touched up chain tattoo, but I didn't expect to use it. I knew what this was; the door to Strangehold. I'd find out what Hawthorn wanted; I hoped it was only a social call, and not some other emergency.

But when I got to the bridge, Hawthorn wasn't there. Rowan was.

He looked like something out of the stories my parents had loved so much, standing beneath the trees, red-brown hair turned golden by the rising run. He was dressed for Faerie, not for overhill, and he didn't look quite real.

"Am I welcome?" He sounded unsure.

"Of course." But even as I said it, I was remembering the strike of his blade, his unnatural grace.

His uncertain smile turned a little sad, as though he

could see what I was thinking. "I have news, though not as much as I'd like."

"Gwen?" He shook his head and I swallowed my disappointment. "Walk with me. We can get some coffee until the girls get up. I know they'll be happy to see you."

"There's no news of your sister, but Elm is back at court. He sent a few things for your nieces." He tugged at a satchel slung over his shoulder. "He asks that they stay a little longer with you, if you are amenable."

"Of course. They can stay as long as they need to. Is he—is he all right?"

"Well enough." Gravel crunched under our feet as we walked. The house came into view between the trees. "The queen may do as she wishes to the ambassador from your sorcerers, but Lord Elm is another matter. His family is old and powerful, and he is not the least of their scions."

I digested the idea; but then again, I had already seen that there was more to my brother-in-law than I had thought when we were underhill. "And what about his daughters?"

He shrugged, and even that was graceful. "Your Association has sent a protest over the disappearance of your ambassador, but the queen has not produced her. Her majesty's temper remains too frayed where humans are concerned for Elm to wish to risk his daughters. And I have told him what the lady of Strangehold said about them. If the queen should discover it as well...no. Best they stay here." He turned before I could think to look away and those too-green eyes pierced me. "But I didn't come here entirely to discuss your relations. Morgan, are we okay?"

I stumbled. "What do you mean?" That was cowardice. I knew.

He sighed, and his breath fogged the morning air. "When we were in Strangehold and you found out I had been the Queen's Blade, you still looked at me as any other person. But after the lighthouse..." He trailed off.

"It was hard to watch." I could see it still, the arc of the dagger behind my eyes, the spurt of Matthew's blood. Red everywhere. "But what was worse was that I chose to do something, and you took that choice away."

"You are not a killer, Morgan." We were almost at the house, but he stopped before the porch. "I was, for centuries. Why should you stain your hands, when mine are already bloodied?"

"I didn't want to, no, but it was my choice, and you decided your choice mattered more." I searched for words. "I thought we were...partners. But if what you think counts for more than what I do, maybe that isn't so."

"I understand." He looked back over his shoulder, toward the bridge behind us. He shrugged out of the satchel and handed it to me. "In that case, I will leave this with you."

"No, wait! Don't leave." He turned back to me, one eyebrow raised. "Look, just because I'm upset doesn't mean we burn all the bridges and walk away. If we're not okay, we don't *get* okay by not seeing each other and never talking about it. We're friends now, right?"

He smiled, slowly. "I would like to be."

"Then tell me you understand why it hurt me that you took my choice away, even if we both know it wasn't a choice I wanted to make."

"I do understand, and I'm sorry." He looked right at me, and held a hand up like a boy scout. "I promise I won't place my judgment over your own again."

"Well," I said, uncomfortable. "Unless I'm obviously wrong."

He took my shoulders and bent down to kiss my forehead. His lips were soft on my skin and that close he smelled of rosemary and green things. My face burned, and when he leaned back I could still feel the press of his lips like a brand. "I am Conant. The queen has said I am to be Lord Rowan again now that I am no longer hidden overhill, but I would like you to keep my name."

"Thank you." From what I understood, this was quite an honor. I don't know if it worked the same for changelings as for full fae nobles, but it was said that their names could be used to bespell them. I never would, and it both shook and warmed me that he trusted that I wouldn't. "I'll be careful with it. Conant."

"I knew you would be." He smiled, and I smiled back.

I turned back to the house. "Come inside, and be welcome."

We went up the steps, and into my home, together.

END

Acknowledgements

Writing a book may be a solitary act, but getting it to the final draft, polished and ready for readers, takes the input of many other eyes.

My deepest thanks to Ben Sears, Stephanie Burgis, Amy Weaver, and Kat Howard for reading early drafts. Their comments helped me sew together plot holes, go deeper with the characters, and scrub infelicities from the pages. Thanks also to Lou Harper, who took my description of Morgan and made a wonderful cover from it.

My family have been incredibly supportive. From a very young age, my parents surrounded me with books, and encouraged my every creative endeavor. And as an adult I am fortunate in my patient children and particularly in my husband, who gives me time and space to write and reads everything I put in his hands. Thank you, Ben; this book wouldn't exist without you.

About the Author

By day, Rene Sears is an editor. By night, (or early in the morning, or on lunch breaks) she writes. She has had short stories published in *Cicada*, Daily Science Fiction, and *Galaxy's Edge* magazine.

Rene enjoys travel and the outdoors and has rafted down the Main Salmon River in Idaho four times. She is also paints and embroiders, and enjoys making things, and aspires to one day unite disparate interests by embroidering a book cover.

She lives in Birmingham, Al, with her husband, two children, and a dog that may or may not be part Belgian Shepherd. You can find out more at www.renesears.net and get a free Crossroads of Worlds novella when you sign up for her newsletter at https://tinyurl.com/renesears

Excerpt from *Sorrow's Son*

Javier has been on his own since his parents died during the sickness that decimated magic users, following a spell to look for other spellcasters without knowing if any survived. When a caster named Morgan and her nieces, Igraine and Iliesa, take him in, he has to hide the secret of his unusual isolated upbringing, desperate not to alienate the only community he has left.

But Igraine and Iliesa have secrets of their own. The wild hunt comes to the mortal world seeking them. Why the Queen of Faerie wants them, no one knows, but no one wants to hang around and find out. Javier flees with them between worlds, finding a rare talent for communicating with fae creatures—though he's sure his father wouldn't have approved of his new hellhound.

A mysterious man claiming to be from his mother's estranged family finds Javier, but does he want to claim the family his mother repudiated? He must choose whether to go to his mother's family or help his new friends—but it may be too late to escape the malevolent gaze of the Queen of Faerie.

The following excerpt has not been edited.

Morgan

It was hard to feel like a properly gracious host when a fae lady was visiting overhill. Not that Lady Hawthorn was a difficult guest—perish the thought. It was just that she was every stereotypical image of a fae: tall, slender, delicate, with pale hair and eyes the color of wisteria. She looked out of place at my kitchen table, but somehow she seemed at home.

I cleared my throat. "Girls, why don't you clear the table while I get Hawthorn some coffee?"

Igraine shot me a black look, but Iliesa rose and started clearing the table. It wasn't the dishes Igraine minded, I knew, but my transparent attempt to talk to Hawthorn by myself. "Hawthorn," Igraine said, "has there been any word?"

"My dear, I should never have sat with you and eaten a meal and said nothing if I had news." Hawthorn folded her hands together, and leaned forward, trying to catch Igraine's eyes.

Igraine stood up abruptly, chair scraping against the floor. I managed to keep from sighing out loud. It wasn't fair to expect my niece to *not* be frustrated with how little information we'd turned up about her missing mother.

I poured a coffee with sugar and a splash of cream—Hawthorn—and another black—me—and led her out into the night. Against my will, my ears strained for the call of a falcon, but only a barred owl called somewhere off in the trees. Only two months ago, I'd have laughed at the idea of having a fae lady as a guest in my house, but I hadn't expected my nieces would be living with me either. I wouldn't have been sorry about any of it if only I knew my sister Gwen was safe.

"Are the girls..." Hawthorn trailed off, curling her fingers around her cup.

"They miss their parents, of course. And they don't think I'm doing enough to find them." An opinion I sometimes shared. I'd done everything I could think of but none of it was enough. Nothing had worked.

"I know you are doing all that you can. Rose has continued to look, but she finds nothing about your sister." Hawthorn laid a hand on my arm, and I let myself take comfort from it. In the distance a dog barked. "Have you heard anything from Rowan?"

I shut my eyes against her gaze, then opened them and looked at the distant stars. "No. Not yet." I worried about that, too. Had something happened to him? Or...did he not want to come back? It was stupid to miss someone so much when I barely knew him, no matter what we'd been through together. Hawthorn murmured something sympathetic.

I wanted so badly not to be the adult all the time, but it wasn't for Hawthorn or Rowan, wherever he was, to take my responsibilities for me. Hawthorn had already helped so much, opening her home to me and the girls, letting them stay there while I had travelled to my spellcaster acquaintances to help rebuild after the Savannah flu and ask for help finding Gwen. No one had been able to help me, and the girls had come back from Strangehold older than they had left. It was another thing to worry about. I couldn't let myself hope too much that Rowan was still looking for Gwen, that *that* was why he'd been gone so long.

I touched Hawthorn's hand, and she squeezed it back. She might not have any answers for me today, but it meant a lot that she came to see us, to listen. I turned back to the house.

"The girls are probably done in there," I said. "Let's go home."

Javier

I'd been evading the monster for three days now, and I wasn't even out of Atlanta. Towering metal-and-concrete canyons had given way to a sprawling expanse of strip malls and highways. This particular strip mall housed a glass-fronted shop with a faded display of black cloth and cards bracketed by iron bars between a vape shop and a payday advance place. A tattered sign above the cards read THE MAGIC SHOPPE in a curly font. I had no real hope there would be any actual casters here, but...I don't know why I stopped, except I was desperate for someone to see me and know what I was.

I surreptitiously touched the lump of incense in my pocket. I had yet to get a hit off the spell I'd cast at least once a day since I left my aunt's apartment, but this place might—*might*—hold a clue. If I could find someone else like me, maybe they could explain why the monster had come after me.

Bells jangled as I pushed through the door. It was musty inside, dark and close, and when I called my spellsight, nothing glowed silver. Except...I went deeper into the shop, following the faintest smudge of light. I followed it to a metal chest in the back of the shop. I tipped back the lid. The silver light inside was pale and gray, but brighter than what I'd been following, just barely. I touched the tiny silver frog on a cord around my neck for luck and reached into the chest.

The glow led to a blunt silver dagger set with glass "jewels"—more a letter opener than an actual knife—but it was pretty, and at one point it'd been imbued with magic. Either it was used in a ritual or it was spelled to do something. I couldn't tell what. The traces of magic were faint with age. Disappointment hit me—whatever magic had touched this blade, it had happened long before the Savannah flu and its death toll on all magic users.

"Can I help you?"

I turned. The man behind the counter was paunchy and a graying ponytail hung down his back. I didn't sense any wards or charms on him. He squinted at me through wire-frame bifocals.

"I was just admiring this knife." I knew how I looked after three days sleeping on the streets, and I probably smelled, but the look he turned on me was more thoughtful than like he was about to kick me out of his shop. My spellsight didn't turn up anything, but maybe—

"There was a fella in here a little while ago, kind of looked like you, asking about...where are you from?"

Grim humor turned up the corner of my mouth. I'd been asked this question a few times since leaving the island. "South Carolina."

"No, I mean—where are you from? Where's your family from?" He waved vaguely at his face. I frowned. "No offense."

"What was the guy asking about?"

"He was looking for his brother."

"I don't have a brother." I set the knife down carefully and ran my fingers over the paste jewels, trying not to think about all the family I didn't have. "How much is this?"

His brow crinkled as he looked at the knife. "Twenty bucks."

"I'll give you ten." It couldn't be actual silver, not for twenty bucks.

"Fifteen." I considered the steadily-dwindling stack of cash my aunt had given me before she left. I really shouldn't spend any of it on something like this—I had no way of knowing when she'd be back. Still, the knife drew me—even old and unused, it was the first link I'd seen to other casters.

"I'll take it." I crossed the store to the counter, fishing three crumpled fives out of my wallet. This close, the guy smelled like patchouli and smoke. There was a display of bongs next to the register. The guy wrote a note in an actual ledger—no bar code items here—and popped a button on an antique cash register to put away the money.

"If that guy comes back, what should I tell him?" He raised faded blue eyes to meet mine.

I shrugged. "Whatever you want. He's not looking for me."

"If you say so." He wrapped the knife in newspaper—for fifteen bucks I wasn't getting the chest—and dropped it in a plastic bag with THANK YOU in red letters.

"Safe travels," he said after I thanked him, and retreated though a beaded curtain to in the back of the shop.

The parking lot had been mostly empty when I walked up, but now there was a conspicuous addition next to the old Cadillacs and rusted Hondas: a gleaming black SUV with rental plates. I didn't know a ton about cars, but I'd been learning since I came to the mainland, and this one was obviously expensive.

I pulled my baseball hat down low over my eyes and cut away from the SUV, toward the road that led back to the highway.

"Hey! Hey!" a voice called from the SUV. I tucked my chin and walked faster, pulse speeding. There was no reason for anyone to be looking for me. My aunt was the only person who knew who I was, and she had flown back to Puerto Rico to be with her pregnant daughter. I heard feet pounding on asphalt as he ran to catch up with me. I whirled around as he reached for my arm.

He was older than me, but not much, and he looked strangely familiar—but I knew I'd never met him before. The circle of my acquaintances just wasn't that big. His eyes widened as he took me in, and his hand twisted up and to the side. I didn't need spellsight to recognize it as the trigger gesture to a spell. Which one? I wasn't going to wait to find out.

Most spells took time to set up, but there were ways around that. My mother had made me dozens of little charms over the years, ways to track me, protect me as I ran wild through the woods. The frog at my neck had been one of them, a *coquí* singing a song from the home my mother had renounced and I'd never been to. It fell silent when she died—all her spells did. I hadn't been able to fool myself that she was still living for very long.

I'd made my own charms, braided threads wrapped around beads set with spells. I was guessing he had something similar on him somewhere. When he started to cast, I grabbed the ratty collection of cords around my wrist. My father and I had had worked out a simple spell of misdirection. The strands of the spell snapped into a complex web that would take him precious seconds to unpick—and while he was doing that he wouldn't be able to see me or get a fix on a spell.

His face contorted; confusion or frustration, I wasn't sticking around to find out. I took off running, ducking behind the row of shops, ignoring the rot-sweet reek of the dumpsters as I sucked in breath. I jumped over a concrete retaining wall into the woods behind the shops, shoving through a tree break for perhaps twenty feet until it opened onto a residential street.

I stopped for a moment, heart hummingbird-fast and hands trembling with adrenaline. A scratch on my face from a branch I hadn't noticed burned. I tightened the straps of my backpack and set off at a fast walk. As much as I wanted to book it, a dirty kid running through a neighborhood was going to attract the wrong kind of attention. I went right at the next intersection, then right again, then left. A mom and two kids were throwing a ball in front of a yellow house. The mom frowned at me; I waved a hello and kept walking.

Who the hell was that guy? What did he want from me? Maybe he'd been friendly, and maybe I shouldn't have run—I was looking for other casters—but then why had he opened with a spell? It was hard to interpret that as anything other than aggressive.

It was weird too, because who would even *know* about me? Unless...maybe he was like me, just looking for another caster...any caster. I shook my head, despair a flat flavor over my tongue. I'd finally found a caster—or he'd found me—and I'd had to run away. But I'd known I'd have to be careful. My father had warned me that there were groups of casters—"My enemies," he'd said, with a sour twist to his lips—that hated him.

My pulse slowed as I walked and there was no screech of wheels behind me. I'd cut right through into a neighborhood, but if he didn't want to abandon his slick car, he'd have to drive around and around to get from the strip mall to here, and the confusion spell should have kept him distracted long enough that he wouldn't be sure exactly which way I'd gone.

I followed the residential street a few more blocks. When I came to a secluded stand of trees at a crossroad, I pulled a lump of incense out of my backpack. I'd been using my little *coquí* to store power since mom died, and I pulled a thread of power from it rather than look for a leyline here. I broke off a chunk of incense the size of the tip of my thumb and cupped it in my hands. I thought of fire, of the spark that jumped when I thumbed the wheel of a lighter.

I hadn't needed a lighter in years.

The incense began to smolder dully, sweet smoke dribbling out between my fingers. It burned against my skin but the pain was only a distraction from the need for a direction.

This was the slow way to cast, not nearly as efficient as what my father taught me, but not nearly as distinctive either, and if the guy—or the monster from my aunt's apartment—were following me, this tiny blip of magical energy shouldn't register.

I had a thousand memories of my father showing me how to cast. I swallowed as a sudden pang of loss surged out of the ever-present ache of grief. I couldn't let it interfere with the spell. He wouldn't have wanted that, no matter how basic the casting. I waited until the smoke was thicker, then focused my need and pulled a trickle of magic from the air. *I need to find someone like me. Someone who will help me*. A lump of sadness or panic threatened to choke me, but I swallowed it down. *They can't all be dead but me and that guy. I need other casters. Show me where they live*.

The smoke wavered, sweet and thick-smelling, then spilled out in a line, ahead and to the west, as if a strong but very pinpointed wind blew it flat. It was a thin line, and not as decisive as I would have liked, but for the first time since I left my aunt's place, it was *there*.

Relief weakened my knees and I stumbled even though I was standing still. I wasn't alone. The Savannah flu hadn't killed them all. *There are others like me, out there somewhere*.

I pinched out the incense. The smoke dissipated until all that was left was the memory of the smell.

Now I just had to keep walking.

One step after another. I headed west.

*

I stopped walking at an intersection and tilted my head up to the heavy clouds. In the days since I had left the magic shop, I hadn't felt watched, either by magical means or mundane. I licked rainwater from my lips and shifted my backpack, trying to make it more comfortable. It was a lost cause.

My sneakers had started squelching miles ago, and I didn't remember the last time my feet hadn't ached. There was no one out but me—no surprise; it was night, and rain had been falling for hours. Reflections of orange streetlights smudged the wet asphalt. There were no cars, no pedestrians.

I shook my head violently, rainwater spattering off the hood of my sweatshirt and into my eyes.

I was hoping to find a place to sleep. The rain came harder, pounding my head and the asphalt with a thousand tiny bombs. My left sneaker had a hole where the canvas was ripping away from the rubber sole, and the wet edges were rubbing new blisters in my ankles. If I could find an awning or overhang—even the door to a store or gas station, closed for the night—I'd be dry. Dryer, at least. I'd slept in worse places since leaving Atlanta.

An image flickered into my head: a small but sturdily built house, chickens pecking in the yard, the smell of shrimp on the boil with onions and corn. Sunshine and warmth. *You can never go back.* The sense of hope that had sustained me since the incense pointed me toward other casters was hard to find right now.

I shivered. The spring air wasn't cold, exactly, but it was getting colder as the sun went down, and I was tired and hungry. There were a few granola bars in the bottom of my backpack, but I'd find a place to stop first and get out of the rain before I ate.

My shadow flared out along the road: headlights behind me. I hopped over the curb, long grass lashing my jeans, and turned to watch the headlights creeping closer, turning the rain gold in the column of illumination. I fully expected the pickup truck to pass by, like every other vehicle had, but it slowed beside me, and the passenger window rolled down.

A woman leaned across from the driver's seat and called out to me. "Need a ride?"

I hesitated.

"I've got a towel in the cab. Tell me where I can take you." Thunder rumbled in the distance, and the sky opened up even more, pelting me with water. I looked skyward, blinking water out of my eyes. She was headed the way I wanted to go. I pulled open the door and swung up into the cab, bringing a wave of rain in with me.

Water puddled on the leather seats. "Sorry," I said. She pulled a faded blue beach towel from the floorboards and passed it to me. I scrubbed with the towel. She was older than I thought at first—maybe my parents' age. My fists clenched and I made them relax.

"Don't worry about it, it'll dry. Where can I take you?" When I had to think about it too long, she frowned. "Do you have anywhere to go? I can call your folks if you want."

"You can't." I turned my face to the window and watched raindrops hit the glass and trickle down like tears. "They're dead."

"Oh hey—I'm so sorry." Her voice had gone soft, gentle. "Listen—I've got a guest room if you want a place to stay. If there's some other family you could call..."

The only other family I knew about was in Puerto Rico, and I couldn't go to them. Of all of them, I only knew my aunt, and I already knew she couldn't help me right now. I didn't know much about my dad's people, not even where they lived in any sense narrower than North America. I glanced to my left. The woman was watching the road, but her mouth was twisted in a concerned frown. I didn't think she was a serial killer or a weirdo.

"Yeah," I said, and in my mind, my father snapped *Manners!* "I mean, thank you. That's really nice of you."

She made a noise like *ffffftp*. "What's your name?"

"Javier."

"Nice to meet you, Javier. I'm Morgan." She put her blinker on and changed lanes. "We're not far from my house. I live with my nieces. We've got a big hot water tank if you want to shower, and I can probably find some dry clothes that kind of fit while we wash these."

Something inside me relaxed. If she was an aunt that took care of her nieces, then I already related to their little family pretty well. She glanced sideways at me and took a right. "If they didn't burn the rice there'll be dinner when we get there, but if they did, we'll get a pizza."

She drove and I dried from soaking to merely very wet. We turned down a few increasingly sparsely populated streets, until we finally turned down a long, graveled drive. The truck dipped and sent muddy water sheeting away as we hit potholes. We pulled up in front of a one-story house with a welcoming yellow porch light shining to greet us. Morgan pulled the truck up close to the front door and turned the engine off. It was suddenly quiet in the cab except for the patter of rain on metal.

"Grab your stuff," she said. "Let's make a break for it."

[illegible] fine with any of these. We've got a bit of hot water [illegible] shower, and I can probably find some [illegible] Warhol's?"

[illegible] she asked. [illegible] about that [illegible] to the little [illegible] wasn't [illegible] and looked [illegible] If they [illegible] the face [illegible] done when [illegible] up.

[illegible] from [illegible] went [illegible] We turned down a few more [illegible] populated [illegible] until we finally turned down a [illegible] [illegible] or [illegible] in front of a [illegible] with a [illegible] close to the front door [illegible] was [illegible] on the [illegible] of [illegible] metal.

[illegible] "Let's [illegible] a break for [illegible]

CPSIA information can be obtained
at www.ICGtesting.com
Printed in the USA
LVHW011515241219
641607LV00005B/685